...ise for Kim Catanzarite

Catanzarite writes prose that is crisp and delectable to read.

THE BOOK COMMENTARY

Staked is a fresh spin on vampires.

RON SKELTON, AUTHOR OF *THREE-DAY WEEKEND*

I absolutely love these characters.

JENNIFER KERRIGONE, REVIEWER

[Catanzarite] creates tangible suspense and . . . prose that's immersive and inviting.

THE PRAIRIES REVIEW

A fine storyteller.

BLUEINK REVIEW

A fabulous read and highly recommended.

ZOE ROUTH, AUTHOR OF *THE OLYMPUS PROJECT*

Also by Kim Catanzarite

The Jovian Universe Series

They Will Be Coming for Us

Jovian Son

Bright Blue Planet

10/2023

To Tyler,

STAKED

From one author to another,

Best Wishes!

Kim C

KIM CATANZARITE

forster
publishing
A LUCY H SOCIETY BOOK

This is a work of fiction. Names, characters, organizations, places, events, and incidents are either products of the author's imagination or used fictitiously. Any resemblance to actual persons, living or dead, or actual events is purely coincidental.

ISBN: 978-1-7359522-7-7 (paperback)

ISBN: 978-1-7359522-6-0 (e-book)

Printed in the USA

Created with Vellum

For those who have spent some time adrift at sea

The sun shall be turned into darkness, and the moon into blood (Acts 2:20).

—THE HOLY BIBLE

STAKED

Prologue

The Year 1724:
500 Leagues Northeast of the West Indies

The lookout lowered the telescope and rubbed his weary eyes. Could he be seeing what he thought he was seeing? He'd been in the crow's nest for hours, his shift nearing its end. An older man's sight tended to play tricks after too long under the sun. He scratched his sweaty, half-bald head, then brought the telescope up and looked again. There it was. This time he was sure: a body bobbed amid a small flotilla of what appeared to be wreckage. The head and arm slung over a wood plank, the lower half submerged in the morning's placid waves.

"There's a lucky devil if I ever saw one," he whispered to no one but himself. Then he rang the bell and shouted, "Man overboard!"

Several crewmen gathered below, murmuring and squinting upward.

"Starboard side. Two hundred meters," he said, taking his best guess.

"There!" One of the crew pointed.

By the time the captain had been notified and emerged from his quarters in the usual wide-brimmed hat and weather-worn finery, four of the crew had lowered the dinghy and fetched the victim. The captain's heavy boots beat a pace across the deck boards, reeking of self- importance as he waited the time it took for them to reboard. With a lot of grunting and groaning, they laid the waterlogged body, broad-shouldered and muscular, upon the deck for inspection.

The captain stayed put, observing from a distance. The first mate, a cranky silver-haired sea dog with a deficit of teeth, pushed his way through the men to get a closer look. "He's half dead, Cap'n, if not all the way."

"Is that so?" the captain replied in an unconvinced manner. A couple of the sailors closest to the victim put on solemn expressions as they nodded in agreement. "Look again," he demanded.

Confounded, the first mate studied the victim. A few seconds passed before he said, "Ah, his chest is risin' and fallin'. He may yet have some life left in 'im, sir."

Suddenly, the drenched man contracted into a fetal position and heaved a lung-shaking hack. The closest sailors rolled him onto his side as the dislodged water gushed out. The man's shoes were missing, as was his cap. He wore no jacket, and his blouse was torn at the neck, exposing a portion of . . . cleavage.

"Well, I'll be," the captain said with a smile that raised his ample mustache. "Seems we have a woman on board."

Considering her cropped red hair, enviable height, and lean-muscled build, it was no surprise the crew had mistaken her for a man.

"What ship did ye take passage with?" the captain asked.

Catching her breath before lying back in exhaustion, she used her forearm to shield the sun: *"Ils sont tous morts,"* she muttered with great effort.

The captain responded with a tilt of his head. "What language is this?" He addressed his men. "Does anyone recognize this language?"

"Ils sont tous morts!" The woman spoke with greater volume and desperation.

A Black sailor who had joined the schooner's crew in Port Kourou, French Guiana, stepped forward. "*C'est Francais,*" he said.

"Ah." The captain took the telescope from his first mate and pointed it at the horizon, giving it a quick scan. "And what does she say with her French words?"

"She says, 'They are all dead.'"

"Of course." He snapped the telescope closed. "If the ship has sunk, she is most likely correct." He took a step forward and spoke to her directly. "I assume your ship was caught in the tempest that passed three nights ago?"

The Black crewman translated.

The woman removed her arm from in front of her eyes but did not respond, her mouth twisted as if caught in a net of distressing thoughts.

"Your ship has sunk?" the captain tried again. "Or maybe you were thrown overboard?"

Again, the translation was made.

The woman attempted to sit upright but couldn't quite get there and fell back. The foot of the sailor standing beside her prevented her head from colliding with the deck. "*Non. Vous ne comprenez pas. C'était le monstre. Le monstre les a tués.*"

The captain turned to the Black crewman, but the man, instead of translating, pressed his lips together and diverted his attention.

"Well, what did she say, sailor?" the captain asked.

The French Guianan shook his head.

"Speak," the captain demanded.

"I believe she is confused," he said.

The captain pulled down on his waistcoat and huffed. "I don't care *what* she is. Tell me what she said. Unless you want to spend the night in the brig."

The sailor cleared his throat. "She said, 'It was the monster. The monster killed them all.'"

The captain, who'd been leaning forward in wait of the answer, opened his mouth as if to speak and then closed it again and grinned widely, his gold tooth making a rare appearance. A few chuckles emerged from the surrounding crew. "Oh, yes, of course," the captain said, with an air of silliness, "I suppose it was the *kraken*." He raised his hands and wiggled clenched fingers in imitation of octopus arms.

The laughter of the attending sailors flickered like a circle of flames around the woman. She pushed herself to a seated position and leaned against the wall of the ship. With a strained voice, she spoke: "*De quoi vous risée?*"

"She asks what you are laughing at," the translator said.

"Tell her it's nothing of concern. We will feed her and water her, and dispose of her at the nearest port."

Perhaps sensing the captain's dubiousness, the woman reached toward him with an outstretched arm. "*Vous ne me croyez pas. Le monstre était plus fort. Vous devez m'écouter.*"

"You don't understand. The monster was very strong," the sailor translated. "You must listen to me."

"*Il avait des crocs pointues. Et, et, et,*" the woman stuttered as she grabbed her own neck with both hands, "*et il a mordu.*"

"He had sharp teeth, she says, and he bit."

Once again, the captain's good humor plumped his cheeks as a smirk overtook his expression. The buttons of his vest glinted in the sun. "He bit, did he?"

"Yes, sir," the translator said.

"And here I was thinking it was the storm that killed the crew."

The woman continued to speak, faster now, and the translator struggled to keep up: "She says the crew and the passengers had been dying for days. Each one of them was found with a similar wound upon his neck. The mark of a wolf or a giant snake, they all said. Then she watched a tragedy unfold: the monster, a giant of a man, attacked a passenger on the upper deck. He grabbed him and lifted him off his feet, wrenched back his head so his neck was exposed— "

The woman had paused in her storytelling, blinking rapidly, as if struggling to withstand the horrible image stored in her memory. It was a few seconds before she spoke again, as if just then remembering where she was.

"She says it happened the night of the storm," the translator said. "She was manning the helm, determined to steer the ship out of danger, but then the monster dropped the man's lifeless body—and laid his gaze upon her. The only choice was to jump."

The captain squinted with suspicion. "This thing with the fangs attacked the ship in the middle of the storm? Why didn't someone shoot it?"

"*Morts*," the woman said, bowing her head. "*Il les avant tous tu*és."

"She says they were dead. He had killed them all," the translator said.

While an uncomfortable quiet fell over the listening crowd, a seagull's cry pierced the sky with a screech. The woman's story had wiped the captain's smirk clean, and his eyes narrowed with seriousness as his crew awaited his response.

He adjusted his hat upon his head and mopped his brow with his sleeve. "That's enough," he said, bringing his arm down angrily. "This woman knows not what she says. Everyone, back to work!"

The men, mired in thoughts of monsters, blood, and gale-force winds, were slow to move.

"You heard him," the first mate shouted. "Crewmen, swab the decks. Lookouts, to your posts!"

"Find out which ship she sailed," the captain told the translator, "then lock her up. We can't have a loon wandering freely amongst us."

As the others went back to operating the ship, the sailor from French Guiana squatted beside the woman and placed his hand upon her shoulder. "It's all right. You're safe now," he told her.

She stared with disbelief and spoke with a fierce determination that accused him of ridiculousness: "You don't understand. *No one* is safe. Not while the monster is still out there. And I'm not crazy."

"What was the name of your ship?" he asked.

"*Le Chanceux.*"

His forehead wrinkled with surprise. "The Lucky One?"

Her face grew long with sorrow. "*Le Chanceux* de Saint-Suliac has sunk to the bottom of the sea."

One

Present Day

A sound like a thunderclap jolted him from his stupor. It was followed by a sudden sideways pull, a tug of undeniable force.

This was not the slow rocking he was used to, the gentle push and subsequent pull.

Was he dreaming? A rush of vibrations surrounded him; the rattles, bumps, and scrapes that shook him seemed to answer, *Non*.

He was awake. More awake than he'd been in a long time.

Still in darkness, though. Still like a mollusk tucked safely inside its shell.

Something scraped above him. Scraped and then knocked and then scraped some more. There was another noise as well: a scratching sound like an animal's claws below.

He sensed movement, dragging, as if some swell of energy

had grabbed hold of him and was now tugging him along. *But where to?* he wondered. Could this be his ascent to the heavens? Was he crashing across the night sky like a shooting star?

Somehow, he didn't think so.

Non, I am not in the sky, he thought.

He was inside of his shell, as he had been for a very long time—as long as he could remember. And being inside a shell both made sense and didn't make sense the same way being alive and feeling not quite alive didn't make sense either.

His shell shook and rattled and knocked, and an all-over glugging noise forewarned of danger.

And then he remembered: his shell was a wooden trunk, and he was in the sea.

Until that moment, he'd forgotten that he was more than just a mollusk inside of a shell. And now, as he collided with the rigid sides of his trunk and heard the clunk of his arms, legs, and head as they made contact with the surrounding walls, he remembered his body and its many parts: *bras, jambes, tête*. The words were coming back.

And then a pulse emerged from the center of his chest.

He had a heart. And it was beating.

He wasn't dead.

His shell contained him, protected him—whatever he was at this point. He knew what he had been when he first entered the trunk that had become his shell. He was a man. A young one. But that was so long ago, before the dark endless days of quiet desolation had descended and his memory had faded.

The jolting movement and strange sounds had set his dormant thoughts in motion. Perhaps this was yet another phase of his odd, dark existence. Something to take the place of the long, purgatorial stretches of nothingness. The persistent consciousness when he had expected to sink into unconsciousness—but never actually did.

He had welcomed oblivion but never quite attained it.

Whatever force acted upon him continued to hammer, shake, and tease him. It wasn't long before an old, hardly remembered feeling reemerged: he *wanted* it to stop. He hadn't wanted anything in as long as he could remember, but at that moment, he wanted the thumping, pounding, crashing motion to cease. And he wanted the gentle rocking he'd come to know so well to return, for his hibernation to resume.

Instead, a terrible crash that hurt his ears ensued.

In his mind, he imagined a tree split in half by a bolt of lightning. In reality, his shell had collided with something mighty that cracked it in half like a walnut. Before he could think of anything else, he became engulfed within the cold, wet shock of water. Pieces of the wooden trunk fell away, and he spun like the vanes of a windmill, remembering what it meant to be in motion, what it felt like to be free.

His body flailed, arms and legs seeking something to attach themselves to, some floor upon which to stand. The water pushed him like a willowy twig cast into a roiling rapid. He didn't like being free, didn't like the feeling of vulnerability. Where was his shell? Were his eyes even open? He didn't feel safe.

He slowly dropped down, down, down until his toes met with solid, sandy ground. Instinctively, he bent at the knees, then straightened his legs and propelled himself upward, swimming toward . . . the light?

The idea of the *surface* crossed his mind along with warmer thoughts that came with it.

Still underwater, his feet kicked on their own volition and soon enough, he broke through. His head emerged, cold and wet, the taste of salt filling his mouth and stinging his lips. His eyes were useless, unseeing, though he soon detected smears and smudges. *Nuit*, his mind told him. Night. Small waves lapped up and struck his cheek. The coolness of wind brushed his face like icy fingers making trails across his skin. The blur of his sight began to clear. Something retreated in the distance. Something moving over the top of the water. Twinkling lights, triangles of cloth waving like ecstatic arms, a thick rope trailing behind like a tail. *Un navire?* A ship? Perhaps. Albeit a small one. White and unusual in appearance. Moving at great speed.

He tipped his head back, and the world brightened. Sky. Clouds. The pinholes he knew as stars. When he saw the moon, he experienced a surge of hopefulness and his heart trembled curiously. The word *grand-père* crossed his mind, though he knew not why. Before he could give it more thought, the water rolled up and over his head, and with strength much greater than his own, it spun him around so that when he bobbed to the surface, he viewed a fuzzy, hulking landscape in the distance.

Arbres, he thought and tried to utter the word, but his throat rattled, strange and empty. The attempt to speak scratched over its surface and made him cough. He pointed himself toward the trees, the ocean nudging him nearer the land one second, then grabbing him and forcing him back the next, only to push him toward land once again. He was at the mercy of the waves, but after a time, he had arrived close enough to the beach that the tips of his toes touched the ground.

Soon, he could press his feet into the sand and push himself forward. His shoulders emerged and then his chest—but when the next wave went out, the water dropped to his knees, and his upper body came crashing down. His hands splashed into the surf, and he collapsed under his own weight, face first into the ground. An incoming breaker rushed over him, submerging him once again. He used his arms to press up and then he raised his head and began to crawl like an infant, *un bébé*, as the water drenched him and he struggled to leave it behind.

When he escaped the sea's foamy grasp, he fell to his stomach onto a crumbling bed of warmth and succumbed to exhaustion. *The sand is warmer than the water,* he thought. And then he remembered his shell, once again, and mourned its loss.

He didn't know how much time had passed while he'd rested. Enough for sand to embed in his cheek and the ground to no longer warm his chest. The waves coming and going ventured far from his toes. When he lifted his head, his neck resisted and his abdomen ached with emptiness. He suspected he'd beached himself upon a boulder, hard and unmoving below him, but when he reached under his chest with his hand, the damp, crumbly sand yielded to his fingertips, and he remembered how he'd crawled out of the sea.

He rolled over and saw the sky with its many stars and bright moon overhead, and once again the word *grand-père* floated through his mind. Something about the sight of the moon soothed him, as did the remembrance of the word, but he didn't know why. His thoughts were random and puzzling, rising from deep places below the years of darkness spent in the trunk. *Why was I in a trunk in the water,* he wondered. *Where am I?*

No answers came to him, just a shiver of unease that prickled like a bout of hives under his skin.

After a moment, he sat up. The terrible openness of the beach and the way the air touched him all over made him long for cover. He wasn't used to this freedom, this exposure, and he didn't feel safe. The breeze and the cold and the sound of rushing water—there was too much going on, too much to see. Where was his shell? He wished it had washed upon the sand with him, though he knew that wasn't possible. It had broken into pieces and left him vulnerable.

What was he supposed to do now?

All at once a terrible rumbling came from his middle and a wave of wanting rose up from his gut like two hungry hands that grabbed at his throat. He turned away from the ocean and scanned the area in front of him. Beyond the dunes, a stretch of woods spread: the tree line he'd first viewed from the water, chaotic with branches, vines, and debris that blanketed the ground. He wanted to go there. Attempting to stand, he planted his feet in the sand, but when he exerted the energy and will to rise, his legs struggled and shook before his knees gave up and dropped him back down.

Perhaps standing was no longer something he knew how to do. He'd been folded into the trunk for as long as he could remember. Would he have to settle for crawling? He tried to get his feet under himself and to stand once again. This time he started to rise but lost balance and toppled sideways. A chill ran over him as he lay prone, and he watched the hair on his arms stiffen like the wiry legs of insects.

He smelled something.

Offensive and yet desirable.

The terrible hunger roiled through the whole of him like the brawny ocean crests that had thrust him onto the beach. The hunger demanded he move. He floundered on his side for a moment before righting himself and beginning a frantic, disjointed crawl: one foot dragging behind him, an elbow giving out. Every hinge in his body resisted, and the movement required complete concentration. All the while this unignorable want spun through him like a bear desperate to hunt and devour.

The scent grew potent as he neared the woods.

His ceaseless craving forced him to scrabble across a path of wooden planks that bridged over the dunes. A spigot at the top of this footbridge awaited, causing him to hesitate. Was it thirst that propelled him? Perhaps dehydration had driven him to madness?

Since he was on all fours, he reached the faucet easily. Why it was built out here and so close to the ground, he didn't know. The handle twisted after a brief struggle that hurt the bones of his palm. He set his open mouth below it and let the water flow, glugging and choking as he filled his body with liquid. Still, he experienced no satisfaction.

The wind changed direction and that same scent tempted him once again. He scuttled from the path and entered into the dark of the wood, mindless of the ground's debris, the stabbing sticks and thorns penetrating the skin on his hands and knees. Moving forward like a dog led by its sniffing nose, he charged through, searching for the source of the strange, beguiling stench.

The hunt led him to a small horse—or no, not *un cheval*—stubby horns grew from the animal's graceful head. A deer, lying on its side, its legs twisted beneath and blood dribbling over its lip. He pounced, the animal shuddering as his hands connected with its warm trunk and his mouth attached to its supple neck. His teeth penetrated the hide, though not without effort, and then a warm, metallic taste rode over his tongue, and that was all that mattered.

He indulged himself as his stomach softened and veins thrummed, his heart quivering with new life. He'd never consumed anything so soothing, so satisfying. His limbs warmed, the nourishment spreading, and his insides filled near to bursting.

He eased back in ecstasy and rested on the ground beside the animal while it relaxed into its last breath.

Go with grace, he said in his mind.

His entire body pulsed in a pleasing manner, and he grew drowsy and calm. It was only a few comfortable moments, however, before his ears twitched at a sound in the near distance —not the rushing ocean waves but a vibration buzzing the air like a cloud of locusts heading his way. He sat up and scanned the vicinity, surprised to find himself no longer within the safety of the wood but just beyond it. Somehow he'd ended up in a cleared space—the edge of a thoroughfare. The kind made for horses and buggies. He paused in the memory and then came upon yet another one: cobblestone roads and houses in rows.

The buzzing became louder, jarring the interior of his ear. He'd never heard anything like it, the sound inspiring him to his feet. Suddenly he had no problem standing, no problem thrashing about in the brush in search of a place to hide. He settled beside a bush, crouched in such a way that its leaves and branches partially concealed him. He twitched when shards of light broke across the trees. In the distance, two glowing orbs approached. Bright white beams that made him squint.

Twin spirits maybe? Or . . . small moons.

Perhaps some kind of magic.

He wanted to get away but hadn't the nerve to run. Instead he cowered behind the bush as the light grew in strength. He hoped whatever it was wouldn't take notice of him. As it passed in front, he saw the creature's full form: a shiny rectangular cart, white in color, rumbling somewhat angrily, with squares of red glowing from its backside. He noted how it moved upon wheels.

It had stayed within the thoroughfare and continued on its way, just like a horse and buggy would have.

What kind of strange place is this? he wondered.

Three

The crickets raged at an astonishing volume. Either his hearing had suddenly improved or droves of insects had descended without his knowledge. But if that were true, where were they? He didn't like squatting in the woods, didn't like the twigs and thorns and other debris that poked and scratched his skin now that the urgency to drink the deer had relented. He'd have to find somewhere else to hide. He needed to get away from this noise so he could think. He longed to get back to the darkness he was used to, the quiet. Maybe he could find a hole to climb into. A hole would be a good substitute for a shell. Perhaps he could dig one. Yes, now that his body pulsed with energy, he would dig a hole.

As he moved over tree debris that crackled and crunched underfoot, he became aware of the waves in the distance, drawing in and out, like a sleeping giant.

Respiration.

In and out.

Like breath.

Was he holding his? Seemed like he was. He took in a

breath of air and purposely held it. Then he continued to hold it while he counted to fifty. And then one hundred.

This didn't make sense.

He didn't need to breathe. So, was he alive?

He'd reached the sand, still warm a few inches below the surface, when another kind of sound surprised him. He jerked back into the brush and squatted, sniffing the air as he detected a deep murmuring. Someone was talking. A low voice. *Un homme*, he thought.

He scanned the area. Two males and a female traveled the beach toward him. They wore unusual clothing and smelled of cooked meat, fire, salt, and—suddenly a sound he remembered. Laughter.

"Hey, you okay?" The closest of the two young men sped toward him now.

He stood, thinking he could still run if he had to, if these people wanted to hurt him.

The girl followed, stepping like a curious cat as she neared.

"Do you need some help?" the man out front said. "I don't think I've seen you around before. My name is Liam."

The words the man spoke weren't the same as the ones inside his head. He understood them, but they sounded very different.

The female stepped forward. The shoes upon her feet—just a sole with a strap—made a slapping sound. *Slap-slap. Slap-slap.* "Are you all right? Did someone hurt you?" She wore a long, full skirt, and her top stopped short so that her middle showed. Perhaps she was *une bohemienne.*

The third person, a tall man with an unruly beard, nudged the girl aside and stepped in front of her, in what may have been an act of protection. "Is that blood on your shirt?" he said with a scowl that revealed a crooked set of teeth. The man pointed at him, his long arm aimed at his chest.

When he bowed his head to observe his own body, his hair

impeded the view. Strange rags hung like moss from his limbs. Rags with dark stains. *What am I wearing?* He crossed his arms over his chest, wishing he might blend with the trees.

"*Non*," he said, the word tickling his windpipe. He grunted, cleared his throat. "I-ya goo—" He stopped there, his mouth mangling what he'd meant to say, which was, "I will be going now."

"You okay, old man?" The bearded guy's voice was rough as rocks. "Why don't you step out here so we can take a better look at you?"

He shook his head, wishing the three of them would leave.

"Temperature's dropping," said the one who'd called himself Liam. "Is that all you've got to wear?"

When he glanced down again, he saw bones in his chest like planks with a series of trenches in between. Why was a large portion of his shirt missing? He took a step back, horrified by his appearance. Was there no place he could hide?

The girl moved forward, her slender hand extended. "It's all right," she said softly. "We want to help." She reached toward him with patience in her dark eyes outlined with thick, inky lashes. She smelled like flowers. Soapy ones.

He hated to think what he smelled like.

"We can give you some clothes, something to eat," she said. "A blanket for the night. Do you have a place to stay? I'm Benicia." She smiled at him, and he had the sensation of her touch even though nothing of hers had touched him.

For the next moment, he hung on to her smile and stifled an urge to draw her close to him . . . and kiss her. He continued to stare, and she did not flinch. He *knew* her. Her pleasant features and golden-brown face brought warm feelings to the surface—good feelings—and then others not quite as good. At once he wanted to embrace her and at the same time, he didn't want her to see him like this, didn't want her to see whatever had happened to him.

"What's your name?" she asked.

Gregorie. The syllables leapt through a dark space in his mind, but when he attempted to speak them, they came out as threadbare and tattered as his clothes, "Gre-gah-wey," more a gargle than a word.

Trying again, he braced himself and focused, pronouncing "Gre-gor-ie," not without effort.

"Gre-gor-ie?" The *gentille fille* spoke slowly, as if unsure. "Is that what you said?"

"Gregorie Babin, *oui*," he said, remembering his full name.

"And you're French?"

"*Oui. Francais.*"

The rough, bearded one moved closer. "That your blood, French fry?" Once again, he pointed at Gregorie's chest.

G*entille* slapped his hand away. "Don't be rude, Paul," she said, her kindness disappearing for a moment.

"Give me the cell phone, Benicia," he said.

She raised her voice: "Not if you're going to shine the flashlight in his face."

Paul's lips curled into an angry grin. "Okay, well, I'm pretty sure the guy's got blood on his shirt. Don't you want to know how it got there?"

The thought of blood prickled under Gregorie's skin, not in an unpleasant way. When he thought about what happened with the deer, he sought out the ground and took a step back. The idea of these people knowing what he'd done didn't sit well. Why had he drunk the blood of a deer? And how? He brought his finger to his mouth and dragged it across the surface of his teeth, stopping when one of them cut his finger. Then he turned and pointed behind himself, in the direction of the thoroughfare. "A deer died over there," he said.

"I knew I smelled something," Paul grumbled as he headed in that direction.

The other two crept closer to Gregorie, joining him in the brush.

The girl touched his shoulder. Everything about her face felt familiar. And kind. *Gentille.*

She turned to the one named Liam and stared with an unspoken intensity.

"No judgment," Liam told him, "but you can't walk around dressed like that. You need to get cleaned up. If a tourist sees you, they'll call the cops, for sure, and you'll end up spending the night at the station. Believe me, you don't want that."

"I had to move it," he said, trying to piece together a reason for the blood on his shirt. "The deer, it had fallen into the—"

"Poor things get hit all the time," Gentille said. "We have some clothes back at our campsite. Nothing special, but they're clean. You can have them."

"Yeah, follow us." Liam waved him on as he and Gentille started out of the wood.

"What is a *tourist*," Gregorie asked, but his voice was soft and weak, and neither of them heard.

He considered running in the opposite direction, thinking it safer to remain on his own. He didn't like the one named Paul but worried that if he ran, they might chase after him. While he hesitated in indecision, Gentille turned and smiled at him, the softness in her gaze urging him to follow.

And that was it. He did.

Gregorie hung back several paces. Pants, he wanted. A shirt too. But he wasn't ready to trust three people he'd just met. He wondered if there would be others wherever Liam led them. He would take the clothing and then dig a hole to crawl into. He needed to be alone so he could think and, more important, remember.

They crossed an expanse of beach before Liam checked over his shoulder, then pointed into another wooded area. This one appeared broader in scope. "It's just ahead," he called.

A narrow trail came into view where walkers had worn a footpath, and Liam and Gentille started down it. Paul appeared from a dark cluster of trees behind him, bursting forth like a small explosion, and Gregorie yelped.

Paul laughed. "Don't be afraid, old man, I won't hurt you —unless you give me a reason to. Hey, did you happen to see the animal that killed that deer?"

"Animal?" Gregorie swallowed. "It was already dead when I found it."

"Yeah, well, it suffered a pretty sizable bite to the neck. Coulda been a dog, I guess."

"*Non*. N-nothing was there " Gregorie stammered.

Paul strode ahead on his long legs, quickly catching up with the others. "There's something strange about this one," he told them in a whisper. But Gregorie heard. He could hear everything.

When he arrived at the start of the trail, he paused to sniff the air. *Danger?* he wondered, certain he'd be able to smell it. Paul was not nice, but he didn't smell dangerous either.

Liam and Gentille spoke in whispers as well. "We couldn't just leave him there," Liam said. "He obviously needs help."

"He speaks French," Gentille said. "Maybe he doesn't fully understand what we've been saying."

"He might be a junkie too," Paul said. "Did you see his full rack of ribs? And he's so pale he's practically green."

"Moonlight does that to everyone's complexion," Gentille was quick to say. "He also could be homeless and suffering from malnutrition."

"I'm sure he is," Liam said.

Paul did nothing to hide his disgust or lower his voice. "I want it noted that I'm against bringing him here. And whatever happens, I'm *not* sleeping next to him."

"I'm pretty sure that will be fine with him," Gentille said. "But I doubt he'll stay with us."

"His eyes are weird," Paul said, taking his voice to a whisper. "He's got vampire eyes. Every movie I've ever seen, the vampire had weird eyes like that."

"Oh my god, Paul, give us a break," Gentille said with a laugh. "I mean, how can you even *see* his eyes in this darkness? You're such a juvenile."

With his head hung low, Gregorie reached the small clearing at the end of the trail and paused at its entrance. The trio stood in front of a strange yellow structure, tall and wide. A lengthy rectangle with many windows. *Some sort of house?* But it had wheels like the thing that had passed him in the thoroughfare.

Liam pushed upon a panel that appeared to be its entry. It eased back, squealing like a *cochon* before opening fully. He climbed up a few steps and disappeared inside.

Behind them, a pile of blackened logs rested in the center of a circle of stones. Their scent was so pungent it stung Gregorie's throat. *Maman had a circle of stones like that*, he thought. And then he staggered internally. Maman? The name had come to him naturally, and yet he couldn't remember. Who was Maman?

Gentille said, "Do you want to sit? I can get you a water or something to eat."

The thought of eating or drinking repulsed him. "*Non*," he said.

She gestured to the strange chair with silver arms and legs. "Sit down."

He did as she told him, surprised when he didn't break through the flimsy woven seat.

"Are you from France?" she asked.

Her voice sounded like music and seemed to seep into his skin. It was as if something inside of him connected with something inside of her. He would tell her anything she wanted to know.

"I came from the water," he said.

"On a boat, you mean?" Paul fell noisily into the chair beside his, then balanced one of his dirty, narrow feet upon his opposite knee and sipped from a silver container.

"My shell broke," Gregorie said, directing his answer to Gentille. "I swam to the surface and saw the moon, and the waves pushed me to the land."

"You swam here?" Paul leaned toward him as he stroked his beard. "Are you saying your ship sunk?"

Gregorie did not like the way Paul's words seemed to accuse. He drew his legs up to his chest and wrapped his arms around. "My shell broke," he muttered.

Paul's laughter revealed a cracked front tooth. "What the hell are you, a turtle?"

Liam, on his way out of the yellow thing, frowned in Paul's direction. "Come on, man, don't be like that." Then he reached out to Gregorie with a small stack of clothing.

Gregorie took it, unfolding a pair of gray pants and a dark-blue shirt. "*Merci*," he said.

"You can change in the bus if you want." Liam tilted his head toward their home. "There's a pair of sneakers somewhere around here too. I just have to find them."

"They're on the driver's seat," Gentille said.

"Sneakers?" Gregorie asked.

"Oh, they're shoes. You know, for your feet."

He would not enter the yellow thing. For all he knew, they would shut him in there and lock the door, a thought that made his heart thump in wild, uneven beats. He wanted to be safe inside his shell, not locked up, so he'd stay right where he was. But why would he suspect them of wanting to do such a thing? They seemed nice enough—especially Gentille—she wanted to help him. Though he wasn't sure about Paul. . . . All of this ran circles in his mind as he raised his bloody shirt over his head and dropped it on the ground beside him. Without hesitation, he threw on the new shirt and then stood up so that he could step into the legs of the pants. He pulled them over whatever strange garment clung to his lower half, ripped and full of holes. In the moonlight, the veins in his legs stood out reddish brown compared to his pale skin, and he was glad for the pants to cover himself.

When he sat on the chair again, Liam came over and handed him the shoes. Then Gentille touched his shoulder. "*Je parle francais un peu*," she said.

"*Bon*." He nodded, remembering all at once that the words in his head were *Francais*. The words outside of his head were something else. *Anglais*. Someone had taught him to speak English. He remembered that much. *But who?*

"How many live in this village?" he asked.

Paul lifted his bony arms and spread them like the branches of a tree. "This here is a village of three, my friend."

"Or, do you mean how many people live on the island?" Liam asked.

"We're on an island?" Gregorie said.

Paul let out a guffaw. "You're too much. Is this an act, or do you really not know?"

Gregorie pressed his lips together.

"Dude," Paul said, "this is Wodge Island, New England's best."

"New England?"

"North America. East coast. Sound familiar?"

"America?" Gregorie asked. *I've never been to America.*

Liam leaned toward him. "There are about eight hundred who live here year round, but a lot more tourists vacation this time of year. It gets crazy in the summer."

Gregorie didn't like that. Eight hundred was a lot.

"Are you here to visit someone?" Liam asked.

"*Non*. I know no one."

"Okay," said Liam as he sat back and bit into what Gregorie assumed was a strip of dried meat. "So, why are you here, I mean, what's your plan?"

"No plan," Gregorie said, wishing the three of them would stop staring at him so intently.

"That's okay," Gentille said. "We live purposefully without a plan too. And you're welcome to stay here, with us, in the bus, as long as you like."

"You are family?" Gregorie asked.

"The three of us?" she said. "No. We just watch out for each other."

"We have nowhere else to go," Paul said, his voice much louder than that of the other two. "We're basically homeless. Like you. We want to live in an awesome place, and we want to be free, but we have no money, no funds. Capeesh?"

Gregorie didn't know what that meant, but he nodded anyway. Paul's dark, accusing aura demanded a response, and Gregorie wanted to appease him.

Paul drank the rest of whatever was in the silver can, then crushed it in his hand and tossed it into a metal bin near the entrance to the small clearing. "Except for Benicia here," he added with a belch. "Her parents are rich. They have a house on the island."

Gregorie sensed disappointment coming from Gentille, and perhaps more than that, a delicateness, as if she were not pleased about what Paul had revealed. And that made Gregorie wonder if something bad had happened to her.

"Why are you not with your family?" he asked.

She gazed at her lap and pressed into the seat's backrest. Gregorie couldn't help but feel that she did not want to answer.

"I can't live with them," she said. "We don't get along. I just . . . " Her words became lost, and Paul picked up where she left off: "And Liam can't become the corporate monkey his parents insist he become, and no one can stand me, in general. So the three of us, you could say, are together by default. Safety in numbers, you know what I mean?" He raised his bushy brows, one of them with a straight line of a scar cutting through its middle.

Paul's blunt manner caused the others to glance in different directions, none of them looking Gregorie's way.

"It ain't all bad, believe me." Paul clasped his fingers together and rested them on top of his head. "Are you on the spectrum by any chance?"

"Oh my god, Paul!" Gentille said with ferocity.

"What is the *spectrum*?" Gregorie asked.

Gentille reached out and touched the arm of his chair by way of apology. "Never mind that. Paul has a rude streak. He doesn't know when to shut up."

Gregorie stood. He had received the shirt and the pants, and had put the shoes on his feet. He wanted to dig a hole, to get back to the dark, quiet existence he was used to, at least until he figured out where he came from and how he ended up here.

"I'm going," he told them. "*Merci pour les vêtements.*"

Gentille turned to Liam. "He said, 'Thank you for the clothes.'"

"You should stay," Liam said with enough urgency that Gregorie wondered whether he would be in danger if he left them. "Paul's a lot nicer when you get to know him."

"I have something I must do."

Liam nodded. “Okay, well, come back when you get hungry.”

“I am not hungry.” Gregorie took a few steps toward the footpath, feeling their attention on him as he walked away.

Before he had ventured far, Paul came after him. “Hey! Wait a second. I wanna ask you something.”

Gregorie turned not because he wanted to but because Paul was tall and scary, and made him feel like he was something unusual to observe.

“How old are you? ’Cause your face is sort of young, but then you have, like, a lot of wrinkles and the veins in your legs are—”

“Christ, Paul, leave him alone,” Gentille shouted from where she sat.

Paul craned his neck and spoke over his shoulder: “I’m merely asking how old he is. It’s not like it’s top-secret information.”

After that, no one said anything, and the sound of crickets filled Gregorie’s ears. With Paul in front of him and the other two beside the firepit, he sought out the ground. “I am a young man.” That was all he could say because it was all he knew.

“In what world can that be true?” Paul said with a laugh. “I mean, can you give me a number? Cause if you asked anyone on this planet who isn’t an infant or suffering from dementia, they would know how old they were, give or take a few years.”

Gregorie didn’t know what to say. He’d already told the truth. He didn’t remember. Maybe he would soon.

“Like, Liam over there,” Paul continued, “he’s twenty-six, and I’m twenty-four. And Benicia’s—"

“Yes, I am too,” Gregorie said. “Twenty-six, twenty-four, something like this.”

Paul's mouth twisted into a laugh. "No. I'm sorry, guy, but you can't be."

The heat of humiliation spread over Gregorie's face and neck, and pooled in his chest. He slumped a little, the heavy weight of wanting the conversation to end piled upon his back.

"That's enough, Paul," Liam said. "He wants to leave."

"*This* is why everyone hates you," Gentille shouted.

"There's no way he's in his twenties," Paul shouted. "I mean, dude, have you checked a mirror lately?"

"I'm sorry for how I look," Gregorie said. "*Au revoir.*"

"Wait," Paul said. "Your shoes are untied. Do you need help with them?"

Before Gregorie could think of what to say, Paul bent in front of him and worked the strings in such a way that the shoes attached snuggly to his feet.

"Oh. *Merci,*" Gregorie said, baffled by this unexpected act of goodwill.

"Can't have you tripping on your own laces," Paul said.

Gregorie thanked him again, then continued down the path, pausing when his new pants slipped from his hips. He pulled them up and knotted the cord tighter around his waist.

"You have nothing to be sorry for," Gentille called. "*We're* sorry about Paul."

"Right, you're sorry about me." Paul had returned to the firepit. "Even though I just caught him in a lie. He's twenty-four or twenty-six, my ass."

"You laughed in his face," she whispered angrily. "You never learn."

"Yeah, well, we can't all be perfect angels like you."

"Please come back and visit us, Gregorie," she called.

Her kindness kept him from feeling bad as he continued on his way, remembering how Maman used to tell him that "kindness is the most important thing."

An image of a petite woman with wide-set blue eyes and a blue dress to match came to mind, and his heart swelled. It was his mother, *sa mère*. Maman. He lived with her. In their home. Wherever home was. A clear image of this woman hovered in his mind—and yet there was nothing else. No sound of her voice. No memories to bask in. No stories to tell himself.

Why can't I remember Maman?

Four

As Gregorie walked back to the beach where he had washed ashore, the scent of the deer met him in windy wisps, still appealing but no longer sending him into a mad pursuit. He wondered, once again, why it was he could draw in air and smell what came with that air, but he didn't need to breathe.

Wouldn't that mean he wasn't alive?

And in that case, what was he?

He settled for both not alive and not dead. After all, his heart beat at least some of the time, and he'd survived underwater in a wooden trunk for he didn't know how long. Much longer, he had a feeling, than most living people would. He wished he remembered more. Maybe if he could get back to a quiet, dark place, it would be like retracing his footsteps, and all of it would lead him back to Maman and the rest of his memory.

Now, where to dig?

He stopped midway between the surf and the small forest, dropped to his knees in the sand, and dug in with both hands. The granules moved and slid as a trench began to materialize.

He continued to work without tiring, as if den building came as naturally to him as it did rabbits and ghost crabs. Had he always been able to do this? For some reason, he didn't think so. He moved mounds and more mounds as if he had shovels for hands, throwing armsful of damp sand up and out an opening at the top. He didn't stop until a space hollowed out around him, a plump belly of a place with cool walls, smooth to the touch. Satisfied, he collapsed into a fetal position at the bottom and eased into the darkness. It was good. Much like his shell, though not the same.

Not much time elapsed before whispers, like air passing through cracks in a wall, met his ears.

And then a brazen voice followed: "He has to be in there. He practically admitted to being a human turtle."

It was Paul. The loud one.

"I mean, what else could it be? A giant sand crab?"

That was the voice of Liam, but Gregorie would not move, determined to remain safe and sound within the hole.

The slap of footsteps brought with it a picture of Gentille's unusual sandals. "Hello? *Bonjour? Comment t'allez vous?*" she said. "Are you in there, Gregorie?"

Her voice raised his ears along with images of her delicate hands and the freckles that crossed the bridge of her nose, like seeds over a crust of bread.

"We're sorry to bother you," Gentille said. "We just want to make sure you're all right. Can you breathe in there?"

"I'm fine," he said, though he'd meant to remain silent so they would go away. "*Merci.*"

"We also wanted to see if you needed breakfast. We have some apples. *Les pommes de terre*?"

"That's potatoes," he said, and Gentille's giggle dropped in and filled the den with pleasantness.

"Sorry about what Paul said yesterday," Liam added. "Right, Paul?"

"Oh. Yeah. I was rude. Get used to it. I'm the rude one. Born without a filter."

"You always use that excuse," Gentille said, "but ADD doesn't make you unlikeable, so don't even—"

"Well, then I guess I'm just naturally a dick." The sound of his grating voice was vulgar, like he'd been at the tavern all day, filling up on ale.

Gregorie didn't care. "I am not hungry," he said, hoping they would leave him alone. "*Au revoir*."

"We're also worried someone might fall into this hole and hurt themselves," Liam said. "Because you dug it in the middle of the beach. It's going to be a sunny day and a lot of people will be here. I could show you a better place, if you want, a beach with more privacy."

Could this be true? He did not want to be around a lot of people.

"Dude, Liam's right. This is *not* a good place to bury oneself alive," Paul said.

"Please come out," Gentille said, and her voice grabbed hold of him.

He couldn't ignore her the way he could the others. He couldn't just turn over and settle back into oblivion. He stretched his back and decided he would join them. Pushing himself to a stand, he poked his head through the sunny entrance the same way he had broken through the surface of the water when he was freed from his shell.

Liam and Gentille sat at the edge of the opening. Paul must have gone wandering. Gentille wore something shiny and brown in front of her eyes. A mask? Gregorie's eyelids closed against the bright light, though he tried very hard to keep them open. He hadn't seen the sun in . . . a very long time.

"That's a pretty amazing den you made," Liam said. "Are you standing, or—"

"*Oui*. I am standing."

"Is it dry in there?" Liam said.

"*Oui*, very comfortable." Through slits, Gregorie admired what he could see of the sky, which was so blue it made his eyes water. He wiped a tear and sand sprinkled onto his cheek, causing him to rub, which dropped more sand upon his face.

"Oh, no, don't do that," Gentille said, brushing the granules away. "Here, take my sunglasses."

He was still in the den with just his head peering out, so Gentille removed the shiny brown thing from her face and propped it upon his nose, pressing one of its skinny arms behind each ear. Everything became soft and rosy, and the tears stopped flowing.

"Better?" she asked.

The urge to touch her came over him, and he reached out but didn't know where to go from there, so he put his hand on her foot, then eyed her sheepishly. She tilted her head in question—and the two of them shared a laugh.

Liam said, "What's funny?"

"Nothing," Gentille said, and turned away, as if drawn to the view of the ocean. "Are you going to come out of there?" she asked Gregorie.

"If you stay here, the kids will no doubt want to climb in. You'll never be alone," Liam said.

That sounded horrible. He needed to be alone. He wanted to remember.

"You know what kids are?" Gentille said. "Those small, adorable humans."

"Children will want to get into my hole?"

Paul had returned by then, and his laughter cracked like shattered glass. Gregorie hunched his shoulders, feeling the assault of the loud one's sudden presence.

"All the kids in town will want to get in your *hole*," Paul said before continuing to a large piece of driftwood that he proceeded to yank out of the sand.

"Paul moves around a lot," Gentille told him, "kinda like a fly that circles and lands here and there. He's always close by."

Gregorie enjoyed the comparison of Paul to an insect.

"Anyway, you should move," Liam said, back to the business at hand. "Someone might trip or fall and break a leg, and you'll end up sued."

Whatever *sued* was couldn't be good considering Liam's tone of voice. "You will show me a better place?" Gregorie asked.

"Of course we will." Gold hoops in Gentille's ears wobbled as she nodded.

Gregorie climbed out of the hole. Liam was about to use his arm to plough a pile of sand in, but then stopped. "I have to get in there and see what you've done, if you don't mind."

"Be my guest," Gregorie said, wiping his arms and legs.

Liam slid in headfirst. "Whoa, man, it's so cool in here. How did you move all of this sand by yourself? Do you even have a shovel?"

Digging the den had come naturally. Which was odd, now that Gregorie thought about it. Why would he know how to dig a den?

A moment later Liam poked his head back through the opening. "Don't worry, we'll help you make another one."

"I don't need help."

"I'll show you a place, over by the cliffs. You'll like it." The sand shifted around Liam as he struggled to climb out. "Paul, you need to get in here and see this."

"I can't fit into a hole dug for that tiny critter," Paul said.

Gregorie observed Paul's long, hairy legs and arms, and agreed. He would not fit.

Liam said, "What about you, Benicia? Last chance to give it a try."

"And have it collapse on me? No thanks," she said.

"You know we'd dig you out, right?" Paul said. "We'd have your back."

"I know," she said, sounding suddenly timid, if Gregorie wasn't mistaken. Then she turned to him and said, "I love the cliffs. You will too."

"I believe you," Gregorie said, and the three of them began to fill the hole.

Five

The walk to the cliffs took longer than Gregorie had expected. The sun's rays stung all of his exposed places—the back of his neck, his arms and face—though his skin remained the same strange shade of white. Without the sunglasses he would not have been able to see. Gentille told him to keep them, promising she had another pair in the yellow bus. While he longed for the darkness he'd relished in his den, the sunlight seemed to energize her, and every once in a while she spun in a circle, the wind lifting her full skirt. Her brown skin grew richer in color, unlike Liam's, which turned red and splotchy. He'd removed his shirt halfway there, and his shoulders became the color of *les fraises*.

In Gregorie's mind, an image of red berries climbed a stone wall along the perimeter of a grassy yard. Perhaps the one outside of his home? The memory went no further.

As they trudged over the sand, the sea breezes tousled his hair and pulled at his scalp. The beach curved to the right, and the cliff walls came into view. "There they are," Gentille said, grabbing Gregorie's hand as she pointed into the distance.

The cliffs, a vibrant sienna hue, stood guard over the

curved cove, and something told Gregorie this was perfect. He would live with the sound of the sea in his ears and the salty warmth of the sun in the air. The sight of this place screamed déjà vu. *I have been here before. Or, maybe not here. But . . . I have lived by the sea.* Perhaps this was where he had grown up.

As the three of them approached the cliffs, Paul walked in the surf by himself, and Liam and Gentille remained a few steps ahead, gazing back at Gregorie every so often with sweat-shiny faces. Eventually the white-gold of the sand gave way to a finer, softer consistency that led to a dense reddish-brown clay scattered with pebbles and bits of broken wood, the ground packed hard and covered with sharp pieces of shell. It would be difficult to dig here.

"People don't come here?" he asked when he caught up to them.

"They do, but not like the other beach." Liam said. "Too windy and uncomfortable. They like softer sand. This isn't the spot I wanted to show you—it's just around the bend, past these cliffs."

"Do you still want to see it?" Gentille asked.

Gregorie said, "*Oui*," hopeful the ground would be softer there.

Close up, the cliffs were taller and more intimidating. A desire to touch their smooth exterior came over Gregorie, so he walked up and laid his palms on their cool surface. A cluster of spindly trees grew in a crack just a few feet from where he stood. He moved toward it and peered into the space. Perhaps it was wide enough to allow him to fit through?

"Gregorie," Gentille yelled from a few feet away, "what are you doing?"

"Careful, there could be snakes," Liam called. "Tell him he shouldn't go in there," he told Gentille.

"Don't go in—" she called after him, but Gregorie didn't see any snakes and his desire to explore overrode any fear his friends might have. He stepped in, passing through the spindly trunks of trees with their skinny branches and moist greenery, and entering a tight space where the surrounding walls allowed just enough room for him to pass. The odd feeling that somehow this was right, that this was something he needed to do, compelled him to continue.

Liam said, "I can't follow him in there, and neither should you, Benicia."

Gregorie continued in a crouched position, bumping into the sides of smooth rock until he reached an open area. It was like a cave, except that it wasn't completely encased. Light filtered through openings at the top. The uneven ceiling was maybe two stories high at its highest point. The mix of cool darkness and gentle, watery illumination created an atmosphere that appealed to him; he felt less on guard and more like he wanted to settle in, to stay. He removed Gentille's sunglasses and his shoes. The packed red clay below soothed his tired feet.

Gentille had not followed him in. "Gregorie?" she called to him now. "What do you see in there?"

As he adjusted to the dim lighting, a log came into view.

No, not a log. It was a trunk. A beautiful wood trunk of the sort he recognized from home. *Home.* He'd lived by the sea, and he knew a person who made trunks? Yes, he knew a man named Guillaume, and that man built . . . wooden things. He pictured tools in an older-man's hands: a saw, a block of sandpaper. Guillaume's hearty laugh and his skin the color of deep-brown stain like he used to color his creations. Was Guillaume related to him? His father, maybe. Or, maybe not. He couldn't remember.

Whoever Guillaume was, he was skilled at crafting wood into furniture and other objects, like trunks.

Gregorie ran a palm over the top of the box. It was a beautiful sight: richly colored and smooth as can be. Could this be one of Guillaume's? It was medium size. The kind of trunk you'd pack with books and other belongings, like clothing and shoes, if you were to travel. He touched it again. The wood felt dense and glassy. Soft as river stone. With metal hinges and fixings for locking it up. He lifted the heavy cover open and recognized its familiar scent. Its empty insides urged him to climb in, pulling boldly at his wanting place. He stepped in with one leg, then the other, then knelt down and finally crouched into a ball. He raised one arm to pull the top closed.

It fit him perfectly.

I've found my shell!

His heart bounced joyfully in the center of his chest.

His body eased into the darkness, and he felt "right" for the first time since he'd landed in this strange place. It was like he'd been walking around without his skin, and now that he'd found it, he would never leave. He and his shell had snapped back together where they belonged.

"Yo, check this out," Paul yelled. "It's a cave. Have you ever seen this? Liam, you need to get in here."

"No, I don't think that's a good . . . " Liam's voice trailed off.

"Stop being a pussy, man."

Not even Paul's crassness could shake Gregorie from his newfound glee.

"There are no snakes," Paul said, "and this might be the coolest place on the whole dang island."

The slap-slap of Gentille's sandals drew near, and her voice sounded frightened when she said, "What is this? It's creepy as hell. What's that . . . wood chest? Where did Gregorie go?"

"Be careful in there, Benicia," Liam yelled from wherever he remained.

Gregorie wished them away. He'd found his shell. That was all he needed.

Just then the top of the trunk flew open.

"Holy shit, dude. How'd you fit in there? I mean, I know you're scrawny, but damn, you need to eat somethin'."

Paul again.

"What's going on?" Liam's muffled voice indicated he had not yet moved from wherever he was outside of the cave.

Gentille's slap-slap of shoes approached. "Gregorie, what are you doing in there?"

He turned his head and met her stare. "I don't need to dig a hole," he said. "I have found my shell."

At that, Gentille closed her mouth and seemed to suffer a spasm. "Is this what you meant? You were in a trunk like this one, in the water?!"

He sat upright and wondered why she'd spoken in such a loud voice. Was it strange that he loved his shell? She must think so, and if that were true, she didn't understand. It had protected him, kept him alive.

She sat beside him, exuding concern. "But it doesn't make sense. You said your shell broke."

He rested his hand on the wall of the trunk. "*This* is my shell. I would know it anywhere." But even as he said it, he wondered if what he said might be untrue. The wood interior didn't dip and give in the same places his beloved shell had.

"I do believe you," Gentille said, as she placed her hand on top of his. Hers felt warm, as if it had just come from the oven. "Are you cold?" she asked. "We need to get you a sweatshirt."

"Holy crap," Paul interrupted, "there's a chain over here, and a lock. They're, like, ancient." The sound of metal clinking came from across the cave, where Paul stood. "Why would someone leave this stuff in here?"

"The trunk is for me," Gregorie said, sensing Paul's reluctance to grant him ownership. "It's mine."

"How could that be?" Paul said, frowning.

Gentille brushed her free hand over the trunk's side. "It's so beautifully made. Don't worry, no one'll take it from you."

"Paul might take it from me," he muttered.

Paul swooped toward him like a cat pouncing at a bird. "Don't worry, old man, I won't steal your crate."

Gregorie veered back. "I'm *not* old."

Footsteps entered the space, and Paul sped toward the entrance. "Liam, finally. Wait till you see this."

"Oh, man, the light's cool in here," Liam said. "Where is it coming fr—oh, I see, there are openings up top."

"Yeah, right. We could have been living here the whole time."

Liam scanned the ground, probably in search of snakes. "I wouldn't go that far."

"Because you're afraid of what lurks in the dark."

"And it's creepy as hell in here," Gentille said. "Am I the only one feeling the creepy vibe?"

Liam said nothing. "Where's Greg—"

"That's him. Right there. *In his shell.*" Paul pointed. "I told you he was nuts."

"Oh, wow, Gregorie, how do you even fit in there?" Liam stopped beside Gentille, who remained seated beside the trunk with her hand over Gregorie's hand. "You must be pretty damn flexible," Liam said.

"It's my shell. It's not hard to fit inside."

"He's a skinny mother," Paul grumbled.

Liam nodded. "Okay, but you said your shell broke. How can this be it?"

Gregorie didn't care how or why. Something he loved had been lost and now it was found. Nothing in this strange world made sense to him, so why should this?

"It *magically* appeared," Paul said, in a mocking tone.

"I'm going to sleep now," Gregorie told them, hoping they'd leave so he could get to the business of reconnecting with the dark silence. He wouldn't sleep, he knew that, but hopefully he would remember. He crouched down and tucked his head in so he could no longer see. "Please close the top."

"You want us to put the lid down?" Gentille asked, her voice soft with worry. "I don't think I can do that. Will you be able to breathe?"

"I will be fine," he said.

Gentille would do as he asked, he knew. Gentille was kind. She cared. Maman would like Gentille, he was convinced. Maman in the blue dress. He only wished he could remember more about her.

"I'll close it," Paul said, and the lid came down with a bang.

After that, some muffled discussion reached Gregorie in muted pieces that he didn't care to decipher, and soon enough the silence settled around him.

They had left him alone.

Six

He allowed his body to go limp, to drop into a place where he could become one with his new shell. This was so much better than walking across the island with the sun burning his skin. He was meant to live in darkness. That's why he'd found this place. Somehow the shell had called him there so they could be together again. He was certain of it.

His mind wandered, replaying moments of the day: Paul's gruff laughter, the ocean's pleasant breezes, the preternatural taste of the deer's blood. Liam's desire to help him mingled with visions of the ocean and the horror he'd experienced when his original shell split open and he'd plunged into the sea.

Then he thought of Gentille and the strange familiarity between them, her hand on top of his, and how Maman would like her so much.

Maman. This time, her name pushed him over the edge. He slid swiftly, as if down a dark chute, out of control, at the mercy of gravity, destined for some deeply buried place.

The image of her returned: silver-streaked hair piled on top of her head with a flower or two weaved in, a dress with an apron, her concentration focused as she ground the leaves of a plant with mortar and pestle. He followed her, this much he knew. She was the leader, and he followed her wherever she went.

Maman. His insides crumpled like paper, and he no longer relished the comfort of his shell. Instead, he filled with longing and emptiness and the illness of guilt. Something awful had happened. Where did these horrible feelings and blame come from? All he'd wanted was to remember, and now that he had, his sadness grew to the size of the cliff walls and threatened to crush him.

Maman! Where is Maman?

~

The Year 1710: Saint-Suliac, France

"Gregoire, come," Maman said, as she rushed through the front door, her purse dangling from her wrist. She still had her thimble stuck to her thumb, and that seemed strange. Urgent. Had she been in such a hurry to get home that she didn't have time to leave the thimble at the seamstress's shop in which she worked? In other ways, however, she appeared as she did every day: pink cheeks, intelligent manner, the happy vitality he remembered.

"We must visit Monsieur Garnier in his home," she said. "He is very sick."

"Oui, Maman."

The boy named Gregoire—who at the age of twelve still went by his proper, given name—stuffed the rest of the bread and cheese into his mouth, ready to do whatever Maman asked of him. He was her helper, after all; he accompanied her on all of her visits.

"Bring the basket," she said as she opened and closed cabinet doors, searching for something, he knew not what. "Over there, in the hall. Hurry. Vivian says *le monsieur* has one foot in the grave, and I'm not sure what I will need to get him out."

"I'm sorry to hear that, Maman." Gregoire hurried into the hall and lifted the heavy basket.

As a healer, Maman used flowers, plants, and crystals, along with rhymes, songs, and strange words Gregoire had never understood. Some of the plants remained soft and green while others took on the colors of autumn leaves and the texture of parched soil. The basket rattled with miniature corked bottles, their contents tinged with scent, and tinted tinctures and tins filled with mushroom parts and the fluffy heads of weeds—all of the things he and Maman had collected from the forest that surrounded their village.

Maman and Papi (his *grand-père*), when he was alive, were the only healers the town had ever known.

When Gregoire appeared in the kitchen in front of Maman, he recognized her far-off, preoccupied expression, the one that came over her whenever she was called to tend to a new patient.

"Even so," she said, muttering more to herself than to him, "there may be something I can do. We can always hope, right, *mon fils*?"

"Yes, Maman, we can hope."

She studied his face before flipping his bangs to the side. "You need a haircut," she said. "Why does your hair grow so fast? Like the rest of you, I suppose."

He loved that she knew him well enough to know every little bit his hair had grown.

Last month, when he had turned twelve, Gregoire sprouted two inches, and now when he stood in front of Maman, he had a direct line into her eyes. He wished his were blue like hers, blue like the sea that surrounded their village of Saint-Suliac, but they were brown, like mud after a storm. Brown like his father's, or so he'd been told. He'd never actually seen his father.

"Something happened to you today," she said, with an air of unexpected pleasure. "It's there, in your mischievous smile."

He often wondered how she could know when something good or bad had happened to him while she spent the afternoon mending dresses and socks and blouses—and sometimes even under things, though he wasn't supposed to talk about that—at Madame Seamstress's.

"I found a bird fallen from a tree, and I replaced it to its nest. Its mother returned, and I watched her give it a worm." He swelled with pride, knowing how adults believed a mother bird would reject a baby touched by human hands.

"And there is more to this story?"

Maman always knew when there was more.

"Michaelangela saw me do it," he said. He found he could not utter the name without grinning coyly. Michaelangela Martineau lived next door, and Gregoire found her absolutely beautiful from the top of her poofy hairdo to the bottom of her forever-bare feet.

"Oh, Michaelangela, *oui*." Maman removed the thimble as if just then remembering it was there. "That explains it."

"Michaelangela thought it was *extraordinaire*. That *I* was *extraordinaire*. Like I had the magic that makes it possible to communicate with animals."

Maman stood very still and observed the ceiling as if calculating the possibility. "Perhaps she is right."

"*Pardon?*"

"You are just a boy and have yet to discover your many talents." She waggled her brow in his direction, and he suffered a shiver from the middle of his back all the way up to his ears. Possibilities did that to him.

"Come now, we must tend to Monsieur Garnier," she said.

He followed her out the door and onto the avenue, warm with evening color as the sun sunk into its bed, unfurling a soft sky blanket of deep orange and pink. The air rushed at them as if urging them to hurry, and his mother led with swift, graceful steps, her small body a combination of smooth curves and slight bones, of light-brown hair streaked with gray threads, some of them loose from her bun and trailing behind in the evening breeze.

When they reached the monsieur's door, worry settled into Maman's jaw and created lines around her mouth.

"What is it?" he whispered.

She hesitated before pointing at the sky.

Gregoire turned. The parting clouds revealed a bright moon like none he'd ever seen before.

"*La lune de sang*," Maman said. The blood moon.

Instead of the usual silver, it was a perfect circle of deep red, as full as full can be, the color dark and ominous. They both startled as Monsieur Garnier's heavy wooden door flew open beside them and a young maid appeared, her complexion shadowed and messy hair venturing beyond the borders of her cloth cap.

"*Bon soir*," Maman said. "I am Madame Babin, and we are here for Monsieur Garnier."

The girl nodded rapidly with a desperate, closed-mouth expression that implied how dire the situation truly was.

Gregoire had never been inside this manor house.

Monsieur Garnier had no need for Maman's help before. Probably the monsieur didn't trust in Maman and her abilities, as many villagers didn't. Maman wielded secret skills, that's what the townspeople believed. They tolerated what she could do because, more often than not, Maman healed the individual who called for her help. Whether they admitted she was responsible for their recovery was another thing.

Of course, sometimes they didn't recover. Because death was as much a part of life as recovery was. Or so, Maman had told Gregoire.

The general rumor, which Michaelangela had once explained, was that Maman was either a fraud who had no talent at all or a woman who harbored supernatural gifts she didn't admit to. Her tools and medicines were either a smoke screen or mystical ingredients no human should dare to wield. Either way, the villagers didn't fully trust her or her abilities.

In spite of this, they called her when they became desperate enough.

Whenever Gregoire asked Maman what her secret powers were, she laughed and swore there was nothing secret about them. "I simply know which materials to use and when," she'd say. "But not everyone can be healed. Sometimes it is simply their turn to die."

Still, save for Michaelangela and her parents, Guillaume and Beatrice Martineau, the villagers didn't invite Maman and Gregoire for tea or dessert. Didn't stop to ask them how they were doing or even gossip with them about the new romances that sprung up each spring. Maman and Gregoire didn't visit most of the neighbors' homes until the owners lay on their deathbed.

Perhaps this was the reason for the villagers' fear. They associated Marguerite Babin and her son, Gregoire, with death. It didn't help that Maman had raised her child on her own. Nor the fact that she'd sent her husband away, and no one had heard from him since. But one thing had nothing to do with the other. Healing (and the mysticism that came with it) was simply her work. Her *other* job. The mysterious skills she possessed put the bread and cheese Gregoire loved so much in his mouth and on the table.

That was all he really cared about at the age of twelve.

Monsieur Garnier's young, haggard maid led them to the bedroom, the air heavy with camphor, clean and cool, in spite of the way the man's face appeared red and sweaty.

Gregoire placed the basket on the table beside Maman and walked to the opposite side of the room, where he would stand with his back to the wall. Maman needn't say a word to him. He'd been doing whatever she'd instructed him to do since he was old enough to walk. Even as a toddler he'd followed her orders because that was his nature. He'd always been an obedient boy.

She approached the old man with the horrid complexion and laid a hand on his forehead.

"Oh, Monsieur." She took a cloth from the bowl of water bedside the bed and squeezed it before placing it upon his brow.

The man's glassy eyeballs opened but did not seem to see.

"How long has he been like this?" Maman asked the young maid. "You should have called me sooner."

"Since last night. We wanted to call, but the monsieur objected." She sought out the floor and a blush colored her cheeks. "He became quite angry."

Gregoire noted a couple of stray pieces of broken pottery at the foot of the night table and imagined the sound of a water pitcher thrust into the wall.

"I understand," Maman said with a sigh. "It's fine. I will do my best. Out of the room, please." She turned and waved her hand. "You too," she told a young man Gregoire hadn't noticed sitting in a chair in the dark corner of the room.

The man stood. He was thin with long legs and a skinny waist, but the labored way he rose from the chair made him appear old and spent. Before making his exit, the man turned to Gregoire: "Please, don't let him suffer more than he already has."

"Of course," Gregoire said with a sedate nod.

The man was Monsieur Garnier's son, or so Gregoire would learn later.

At the moment, Maman pored over her basket, making that ticking sound with her tongue as she selected the items she would need. With hands full of dried plants and exotic herbs, she said, "Draw the curtains and light the candle."

She meant the black candle. The one used for those very near the end. Gregoire located it and the plate he would set it in. Then he went to each of the windows and dropped the curtains one by one. When he reached the third, he glanced through the mottled glass at the blood moon casting wicked red streaks across the evening sky. Its beauty could not be denied, and as he lingered upon it, he sensed it wanting to reach out to him, as if he and it shared some unspoken connection—and that made Gregoire want to hide.

Maman was already muttering her strange words and phrases when he set the plate on the bedside table and lit the candle. The melted wax dropped in fat spatters upon the plate's center before he stuck the base of the candle into it, applying the pressure that would convince it to stick.

"Ohhh." Maman groaned and pulled back from the patient, as if suffering a sudden pain.

Though this was not the norm, Gregoire stayed where he was, beside the window. He'd learned long ago that Maman tolerated no interference while she worked.

Then she gasped a breath and placed a hand upon her

chest. “This is . . . *mon dieu* . . . ” She struggled to breathe. Her face became as red as Monsieur Garnier’s.

Gregoire rushed to her side. “What is it? What’s happened, Maman?”

Her lashes fluttered, and he feared she might faint as she struggled to draw shallow sips of air. “I’m all right.” She swallowed and made a choking sound. “It is he . . . who is not . . . all right.”

Gregoire eyed the man and his raw, red cheeks, and the way he shuddered and grimaced, causing his forehead to furrow.

Maman fell back a few steps and dropped into the armchair in which Garnier’s son had previously sat. Finally, she pulled a full breath of air, gasping the way one does after being underwater for too long. “He is stuck,” she said, coughing her way back to her ordinary complexion.

“Stuck?” Gregoire pictured the man’s body deep within a circle of quicksand, trying desperately to depart the voracious mud puddle but only rising a few inches before being sucked back in. “We can pull him,” he said matter-of-factly because this seemed the obvious solution.

“Pull him?” Maman asked in a skeptical tone.

“Like this.” He stepped up to the man and put both of his arms out straight, one on either side of the Monsieur’s head, palms down. Slowly, as if they were mechanical limbs set on automatic, his arms began to rotate, from palms down to palms up and then back again. His eyes closed, and he hummed with each exhale. Why he was doing this, he did not know. A strange sort of energy bubbled like a simmering kettle inside his body. It occurred to him that his actions may not have been of his own doing. He raised his palms and lowered them, continuing to hum, all the while wondering if he were doing it “right.” And all at once, Monsieur Garnier grabbed around his wrists.

Startled, Gregoire opened his eyes and saw . . . nothing. The man was not gripping his wrists, nor touching any part of him. He lay motionless in his bed, as he had before Gregoire so much as approached. And yet Gregoire felt Monsieur Garnier's fingers grasping most strenuously. He closed his eyes once again and began to pull up and back as if he were reeling in a hooked fish, straining the way he would if the man truly had been embedded in quicksand. He pulled, groaning a little, his breath becoming labored.

From the chair behind him, his mother whispered, "What are you doing, *mon fils*?"

He kept at it. As the pulling became easier, he opened his eyes and a glowing light appeared within the man's complexion. A moment later, it levitated, becoming a halo that ringed his entire body, a wisp of gold that surrounded him and grew brighter as Gregoire continued to pull. Suddenly, there was no resistance at all. Gregoire raised his arms as high as he could, and the glowing, shimmering ghostly shape emerged fully.

It hung in the air for an elongated moment and then, like the flame of a candle, flickered and went out.

Gregoire stepped backward and stood beside his mother as he experienced a dazed gladness unlike any he'd ever known. He stared at the space where the light had hovered a moment before.

Maman grabbed both of his hands. "Gregoire, what happened? What have you done?"

"Did you not see?" he said. "The glowing slip of . . . the shimmering gold . . . " He could tell by her questioning expression that she had seen nothing. "It was light," he said. "Light that came from Monsieur Garnier."

Motionless, with her attention fixed upon his face, she nodded as if she understood. "I thought so," she said.

Together they observed the dead man whose complexion

no longer appeared sick and red, but neutral and at peace, his lids at rest and lips flat across his face.

When his son reentered the room, Gregoire met his gaze and said, "I helped Monsieur go. I made him unstuck."

The man nodded solemnly. "*Merci*," he said. "I will never forget."

~

As they headed down the road toward home, giddiness slipped out of Maman in the form of small whispers. "I cannot believe this," she said, smiling to herself. "I always knew you were special. But an angel of death? *Mon dieu*." She chuckled to herself.

The cool air whispered in Gregoire's ears as if welcoming him into the night.

"Just like Papi." Maman pointed at the moon overhead, still gleaming like red ice in the sky, though no longer quite as intense and frightening. Just beautiful. The cobblestones clacked underfoot, and Maman, with her arm draped across Gregoire's shoulders, drew him close. She kissed his cheek, and he produced perhaps the biggest smile ever.

"Did your grandfather tell you the story of why the moon is so bright?"

Gregoire shook his head, his bangs falling into his eyes again.

"Only the purest of souls become one with the moon. The souls of people like your grandfather, who was always there for us, no matter what. He was the best sort of man. As good as they come," she said. A flicker of hostility shot through her words, and Gregoire figured she was once again comparing his honorable grandfather to his dishonorable father, Marcel.

Marcel, Gregoire had learned through bits and pieces randomly revealed by his mother, was not the sort to light the moon. Hence the reason she demanded he never return to Saint-Suliac.

"Your grandfather helped people the same way you can help people. I do not have these skills. Do you realize this?"

"Maman, your skills are many," he said, "and très powerful."

"Not like yours," She booped his nose. "You have a special gift, and one day, after you pass, your soul will brighten the moon as well."

"Will it be red then too?"

"Red, white, dark or light," she said, "it does not matter. The moon is the moon."

He relished a deep breath that blossomed into a smile upon his face. He hoped he would live up to her prediction. This strange new ability had lay dormant within him like a new language waiting for him to speak. It wasn't his doing—he'd done nothing to earn this gift—and yet his chest puffed with pride all the same. "If you say so," he told her. "For you and Papi, I will do my best to help others."

Her countenance brightened, and he sensed her pride in him.

"Good," she said. "And we shall tell no one."

This was something she often said, so he didn't think much of it. Gregoire's second-best talent was his ability to keep secrets.

Maman grabbed hold of his hand and began to walk faster until finally they were skipping. She was euphoric and silly, joy rising from her like heat from an oven. When they arrived at the house and she searched for the key in her purse, a knock on the window next door made Gregoire jump. He spun around. Behind the glass stood his best friend, the beautiful Michaelangela, bubbling with her usual mischievousness.

"May I go next door, Maman? Monsieur Guillaume promised an English lesson tonight."

"Of course," she said. "But not too late. You must never overstay your welcome."

THERE WAS something even prettier than usual about Michaelangela that night; a sort of glow that rose from within and gave her cheeks a pink hue like the iridescent interior of a shell. She'd inherited her father's tawny Caribbean complexion and deep-brown hair, which she wore in a mushroom pouf on top of her head secured with a ribbon headband. They were born neighbors, and for as long as he could remember, Gregoire had found her and her simple white cotton dresses and bare feet, heavenly. Her mother, a fussy French woman named Beatrice, forever reprimanded Michaelangela for not wearing shoes, not that her efforts made any difference. "Barefoot forever!" Michaelangela often shouted behind her mother's back.

That night Michaelangela led Gregoire through the house, and they exited the back door into the courtyard and its stone path to Guillaume's workshop, the place where he turned raw wood into furnishings and cabinetry fit for a king.

Michaelangela glanced at Gregoire over her shoulder as they hopped from stepping-stone to stepping-stone. "You seem different tonight," she said.

He couldn't help but grin. *Did it show?* Did he *look* like an angel of death, and if so, what was it that gave him away?

"Happier than usual," she specified, squinting as she observed him. "Is it because of the bird?"

He'd almost forgotten about the baby bird he'd saved that morning. "I *am* happy about that," he said.

"So, I was right? You're magic. Just like your mother."

He pressed his lips together to stop from laughing. He

loved that Michaelangela thought him special, and she didn't even know that he had released Monsieur Garnier's soul.

"I mean, I'll like you either way," she said, gazing at the stars instead of at him when she spoke, "whether you're magic or not." And then she backtracked a couple of stepping-stones until she was directly in front of him, her full lips only a bird's-egg width away from touching his thin, regular ones. "Because I like you," she whispered, the words tickling his insides. Then she turned away and bounced ahead once again, hopping from stone to stone like a rabbit would.

Stunned by this announcement, Gregoire called after her: "I like you too," though the sentiment arrived somewhat stiff and forced because he'd felt obligated to give a response, though he truly did like her. He actually *loved* her. He just never had the courage to say so out loud.

They reached the workshop, where Guillaume sanded the leg of a chair under the glow of several strategically hung lanterns.

"Papa, look who's here an hour late," Michaelangela said, feigning disappointment.

Monsieur Guillaume Martineau was the kind of man who seemed perpetually happy—his round, smiling face was wide and full like the rest of his body. "I'm glad Gregoire has come nonetheless. You're both going to enjoy this evening's les—"

"I think Gregoire is magical," Michaelangela interrupted.

Guillaume tilted his head. "Is that so?" He winked in Gregoire's direction.

Remembering Maman's words to "tell no one," Gregoire hoped Monsieur Guillaume wouldn't expect him to accept or deny the magical part of his daughter's statement.

"And that we should perhaps marry one day," Michaelangela added.

Her father bowed his head, his shoulders bobbing with a

soundless chuckle. “You’re especially giddy tonight,” he said. “What have you two stinkers been up to?”

“Stinkers!” Michaelangela shouted with glee.

“What is *stinkers*?” Gregoire said, glad to have the distraction from Michaelangela’s announcement concerning their possible nuptials.

Guillaume put the piece of wood he’d been working on aside. “*Stinkers* happens to be the English word of the night.”

The three of them giggled, and the air around them grew warm with silliness.

“That’s almost as bad as last night’s word,” Michaelangela said. “*Gory*, I think it was. Greg-gory missed that one—" She covered her mouth after this mistaken pronunciation of his name. “I mean Gre*goire* missed it. I’m sorry,” she shouted just before doubling over with suppressed laughter. A moment later, she stood straight, and with a comically sober expression, said, “But I like that, don’t you? If you rearrange the letters of your name, you get Gregorie.” She hovered before him, urging him to find it as wonderful and humorous as she did.

“Gregor-ie?” he asked, not sure he liked it.

“Gregorie *est* très gory.” Her face lit up with glee. “G-o-r-i-e!”

The idea so delighted her that he couldn’t help but grin in response. “And *gory* means what?” he asked, not sure he wanted to know.

“Gruesome and bloodthirsty, savage and frightful. That’s what you told me, right, Papa?” Michaelangela spoke as if it were the coolest thing in the world to have a name that implied such characteristics.

“Yes, that’s correct,” Guillaume said, “except for the spelling.”

“Gregorie,” she said again, with a playfully devious tone. “That’s your new name. No more of this boring Gregoire stuff.”

"Okay," he told her, deciding he could live with it but only because *she* had made the suggestion. For anyone else, the answer would have been *non*.

"And now, if you're about done with that," Guillaume said, with a trace of impatience, "we will memorize the definition for *stinker* along with a few other phrases I have prepared for you. *D'accord?*"

"*D'accord*," the children answered.

"And later, if you're really good, I'll show you the special wood I've purchased for my new, very rich client who needs two trunks made. It's *extraordinaire*."

Gregorie remained safe in his shell, where memories of his childhood flitted in and out of his mind like birds come to feed on bread crumbs left at the foot of a tree. Maman, Michaelangela, Guillaume: they all lived inside him. All of them close enough to touch. *They* were his home.

Thinking the word *home* made him long for Saint-Suliac. He remembered all of the houses lined up in a row, and the flower boxes overflowing with petals of blue and white, yellow and lavender, and the courtyards behind the houses, the trees and the birds singing from their branches. He remembered developing his skill of knowing when the dying person's soul wanted to break free but could not find a way out of the body. The way this talent grew within him over the years as naturally as the way he'd grown two inches at the age of fourteen and two more at sixteen. He didn't know why he'd developed this ability or how, the same way he didn't know why these memories of Maman and home had come back to him once he'd settled into his shell.

Maman healed the villagers with dried flower petals and

leaves and eggshells and crystals. He sensed that she did other mystical things as well, but he couldn't precisely put his finger on them. Had she made his father disappear? Marcel had left them when Maman had asked him to. Gregorie was still a baby, or so that's what Maman had always told him. It was for the best, she'd said. So, why this feeling that she had done something to make him disappear?

Perhaps one day he would remember more.

That night in the shell, he had not slept because he never slept, never quite achieved unconsciousness. He didn't sleep just like he didn't breathe. That's why he feared he was dead. But he wasn't dead, was he? He was still here. Still thinking and moving, still remembering.

How he missed Maman! He needed to go home, to get back to Saint-Suliac. Why had he ever left?

He rounded his back, and his shoulder blades connected with the top of the trunk. From there, he pressed upward. *Mahogany*, he thought, as the cover opened. He loved his shell. The soft, dense, impenetrable feel of the wood. Without his shell and the darkness it provided, he would not have remembered Maman and the village, and what had happened with Monsieur Garnier and the fact that he helped souls leave their body.

As soon as he rose, the terrible hunger reared up within him as it had when he'd first emerged from the sea. Suddenly he could think of nothing but this awful need. A need for what, he wasn't ready to admit. Maybe this time it would be water . . . or fruit? Whatever it was insisted he get up and hunt.

As the craving crashed through his limbs and caused his hands to shake, he tried to hold it at bay. He wanted to run, and he wanted to deny his desire to run, his desire to seek . . . whatever it was his body wanted to devour. He hoped it would not be the blood of a deer. He doubted he'd come upon another dying animal, and then what would happen? Would he kill one to satisfy his need?

The thought both aroused his senses and made him gag in equal measure.

He considered crawling back into the shell and closing it tight. But tight wouldn't be enough to keep him contained. It would have to be locked, chained, bolted. The need throbbed and burned and threatened to shake him apart.

Before he knew it, he'd passed through the short tunnel that led to the vines and slender trees that grew within the cliff walls. He had to twist sideways in order to scrape through, the leaves of vines leaving dewy trails of moisture upon his skin. The heart in the center of his chest began to bang against his ribs like an angry neighbor demanding his attention. When he reached the outdoors, he squinted severely. He'd left without Gentille's glasses, and the sunlight dazzled him with sparkles and trails. Using his hand like the brim of a hat, Gregorie walked half blind across the beach. He'd also forgotten his shoes and the sand burned like coals.

A brisk breeze slid down the dunes, and he sensed something indescribable that seized his attention. And now he moved in that direction without thought, losing control to the horrible wanting, knowing he would go wherever it led him.

Climbing the dunes, he stepped upon yellow flowers that left the barbs of thorns in his feet, but he was so intent on finding what he desired that he didn't so much as pause. The hunger led him toward a house. Light-gray shingles, bright-white trim. He hopped a weathered wooden fence and ran straight into a garden with a patio and a stone firepit that flamed. There, on a table, a slab of meat the size of a lamb's leg rested on a white tray puddled with red liquid.

With one hand, he pushed the cold slab of meat off the tray and onto the tabletop, where it thumped and rolled to a stop. With the other hand, he lifted the tray, tilting it so the red juices flowed into his mouth.

His eyes rolled back in ecstasy, and his heart swelled within his rib cage. When he gulped the last swallow, the wanting eased, and he hung suspended, as if stunned, feeling the urgency fade and the satisfaction throb like warm pleasure through his veins.

A portion of his upper row of gums pinched and seemed to . . . want to move. Why this would be, he had no idea. But he was pretty certain one of his teeth may have been pressing aside the others. Soon this strange, growing tooth poked out of his mouth and bumped into his upper lip. And then the same process occurred on the opposite side of his mouth. The pair of these new teeth met his bottom lip and pierced it.

He touched one of them with his finger and suffered a small cut.

What is happening to me? Why am I—

The sound of a squeaky hinge followed a muffled scream, startling him out of his introspection.

A woman wearing a broad-brimmed hat, her arms flaccid with age, dropped a silver bowl that clanged against the ground as she covered her mouth with both hands. Gregorie replaced the tray upon the table and ran, leaping to the top of the smooth staked fence and whisking himself over. He landed on the other side in the hot sand. Granules flew as his limbs flailed, his feet taking too long to gain traction before he scampered down the dune. He needed to get back to the cave, to his shell where no one would see him. Where he could be alone. And safe. Where he could figure out what was happening to him—and his teeth.

"Wait! Wait," someone called.

Une femme. Was the woman chasing after him?

"Wait!"

This time he thought he may have recognized her voice, so he risked a glance over his shoulder.

"Gregorie!"

It was Gentille. *Dieu merci.*

With the sun blazing a trail across his shoulders and the bright light blurring his vision, he sped around the bend that led to the cove and then came to a stop in the shade of the cliff wall. All at once he realized that he should have been panting but was not. He could have continued to run without a problem. He had not lost his energy or his breath.

Because I don't need to breathe, he remembered.

When Gentille reached him, she doubled over, hair falling around her face, skin sparkling with perspiration. She smelled of sunshine and salt. "Are you okay? Why were you running?" she asked.

The blood he had drank pulsed like hot water through his arms and legs. He would have liked to have more, but at least he'd satisfied the need enough to regain control of his body. At least he was able to stand still, to listen to Gentille and think of other things. And his teeth had retracted, no longer bumping his bottom lip.

"She's not chasing you," she said.

He squinted at her. "Who?"

"The woman who came from the house. I saw you with the tray in your hands."

"Oh." He grimaced, fearful of what might happen next.

Gentille moved closer. Her voice softened. "I followed you. I was on my way to the cave to see how you were, but I saw you when I passed over the dunes, and I . . . watched you."

He sought out his feet, partially covered in sand, and bowed his head like a misbehaved child. "I didn't do anything," he said. A gust of wind came up the beach and blew his long bangs to one side.

Gentille touched his shoulder and when he lifted his head,

her expression reached out in a way that told him she understood. What she could have understood, he wasn't sure. Unless she needed blood too. Though he doubted that was the case.

"We have food if you're hungry," she said. "You don't have to steal. We're more than happy to share."

"I wasn't stealing," he said quickly.

She maintained their connection. "I saw you with that tray in your hands, and it's okay, I won't tell anyone."

He didn't know what to say, but he didn't want her to think he was stealing, so he had to say something.

"You must be very hungry. I get it," she said, with a nod. "What was it that you ate, anyway?"

"I only drank something, and—" he stopped short. He couldn't tell her what it was.

She leaned in, encouraging him to "go on."

"It was not something I could help."

"Of course. You were probably very thirsty. We should have left you with some water."

He wanted to tell her the truth almost as much as he'd wanted the blood. "*Non*," he said, "that's not it. I don't want water."

"Oh. So, soda or juice, or something?"

He pressed his lips together, afraid to speak. "My body," he said with a tremor in his voice, "it does what it wants. I have a terrible need."

Her eyebrows came together. "What does that mean?"

"Like thirst, but not for water." He rubbed his nose and then crossed his arms over his chest. Then he touched his hand to his mouth to make sure all of his teeth remained covered.

"Do you mean alcohol?"

"Alcohol? *Non*."

Her eyes lingered on his face as if she might find an answer to her questions there. "Wait a minute. What did you drink?"

All of a sudden she was whispering instead of speaking normally. "That woman was about to cook something. Was it *blood* that you drank?"

He shifted his stance, one way, then the other. The wind came up from the ocean again and whistled as it crossed the cliff walls. He didn't know what it meant to drink blood, but Gentille seemed to think only awful people did so.

"You drank blood," she said, recoiling as if repulsed. "Oh my god, Paul was right. You're a vampire."

Gregorie felt his forehead scrunching as he mirrored Gentille's shock. "What is a *vampire*?" Then he remembered Maman's words, how she'd called him an "angel of death," and he flung them at Gentille: "I'm an angel of death, an *angel*, not a vampire."

"An angel of death," she said, and he could see the words tumbling in her mind. "Isn't that the same thing?"

"Maman said I was an angel," he insisted. "Maman never lied."

Gentille squinted at him. "A vampire is a person who drinks blood, usually the blood of humans—until they're *dead*."

"I don't want to drink the blood," he said, his voice rising in volume. "It only happened twice." He grabbed his head with both hands. "I don't know why I did it. I must be ill."

Gentille took several quick steps backward, suddenly eager to put space between the two of them. When her foot landed on a piece of driftwood, her ankle turned and knee buckled, and she ended up on her back in the sand.

Gregorie rushed over to extend a helping hand, but stopped when he saw how this action painted a picture of horror upon her face.

"Do you want to drink my blood?" she shouted, her mouth frowning as though she might cry.

"*Your* blood?" He retched internally at the disgusting thought. "*Non.* Never."

"Are you sure?"

"I do not want your blood, I promise."

Slowly she sat up, her anxious breaths losing steam. "So, I don't need to be afraid of you?"

"*Non*, please. I would never harm you." He stepped forward in a careful manner, then squatted in the sand beside her. "You're a good person. You have always been kind to me. And Maman would like you very much."

Just like Maman liked Michaelangela. It dawned on him that Gentille resembled Michaelangela.

"Your mother?" she asked. "Did you just say your mother would like me?"

"*Oui.*"

"Okay, but . . . I still don't get what's going on."

"I will never drink your blood," he said.

She laughed a little. "I do feel like I can trust you. Somehow, I feel like . . . we understand each other."

"I do too!" He tempered the urge to embrace her.

"And I'm much better at knowing who to trust than I used to be," she added.

He nodded as if he understood what she meant, though he did not. Now was not the time to question.

"How did this happen to you?" she asked, shaking her head as if she couldn't imagine.

He wanted to tell her. He felt the answer leap up and show itself before disappearing back into the folds of his brain.

"Do you even know how you got this way?"

Again, he felt an answer flash through his mind, appearing for a fleeting moment and then slipping away. "I should know," he said, bending over to pick up a shell. "I *want* to know."

"Well, you must have been bitten by a vampire."

He grinned, unable to stop the laugh that sprang out of his mouth like a cough.

She glared in response.

"Oh," he said, flattening his amusement, "you are not joking?"

"To become a vampire, you have to be bitten by one," she said with confidence.

Someone had bitten him? A vampire, no less? A dog or a horse, he could understand. But a vampire? How could that be? "*Non*. I have not been bitten. Not by anyone. Are you certain this is how it happens?"

"You would have to be bitten by a vampire, and then you would have to drink the vampire's blood."

"Oh, *non, non, non*, that cannot be," he said with a chuckle. "I have never met a vampire, and if I had, I promise I would never bite him or drink his blood. *Ce n'est pas possible*."

"Well, I don't know any other way," she said, in a grave manner.

She continued to stare at him, steadfast in her seriousness. For her sake, Gregorie tried to remember a scenario in which he drank the blood of a vampire. It was pretty ridiculous, considering he would never drink human blood—or even blood from someone he'd mistaken for human.

"I'm sorry, but the thought is repulsive to me. It must be something else."

She pointed at him, then tapped her bottom lip with her finger. He assumed one of his teeth must be exposed, but then she said, "Maybe you don't remember because it was a seriously traumatic event. Trauma has a way of making a person forget."

Perhaps she spoke the truth, though he doubted whatever made him this way was as frightening as Gentille implied. He would be more likely to remember something scary than he would be to bury it in the depths of his mind.

"How do you know about this thing called 'trauma'?" he asked.

The question caused her jaw to clench and then her chin twitched, and he thought she might cry. "Sorry, sorry, Gentille," he said, as he searched for something else to say. "Where do the vampires live?"

She placed a hand on her chest and said, "My name is Benicia, you know that right?"

He nodded.

"I just wanted to make sure because you keep calling me—"

"Gentille. It means *kind*. You have been so kind to me since the night we met, and I started to call you Gentille in my mind, and now that is your name." He placed his hand on his chest. "For me. Is this all right?"

"Oh," she said, and some pink warmed her tawny cheeks. "That's really lovely. You're so different from everyone I know. Maybe that's why I like you so much."

He smiled all the way to his heart. No one since Michaelangela had said something so sweet to him. Or, so that he remembered. It was possible that he'd forgotten quite a lot. "I feel the same way," he said, his shyness pulling his gaze toward the horizon.

Gentille planted her hands on her hips and said, "Well, I don't know where vampires live. France, maybe? I've never met one. You're the first, and you're French, so that would make sense."

He didn't like that answer, and though she spoke very nicely and he trusted her, his insides knotted with irritation. "I am an angel of death. Maman told me so."

"Okay," she said. "So, why did I see you drinking blood, then?"

He had wanted it. He couldn't stop himself. His body led him to it. But he wouldn't say these things out loud. His shoulders stretched upward as he held back the words he couldn't say. "You don't have to fear me. I am a good person."

The bangles hanging from Gentille's ears swung back and forth as she nodded. "I know you are."

Some warmth spun through the center of his chest.

"Believe me, I know *waaay* scarier people than you." She seemed to want to say more, but when he gave her his attention, she averted her eyes. Whatever had happened to her must have anchored itself deep inside, like the roots of a tall tree.

"Can we keep this secret?" he said.

She answered more seriously than he'd expected her to: "I'm the queen of keeping secrets."

"Please don't tell Paul about me. Paul does not like me."

"That's not true. Paul's just rough around the edges. But I won't tell him if you don't want me to."

"Or Liam," he said, giving her a pointed look.

She wasn't as quick to agree to this.

"But you can trust Liam," she said. "I know from experience."

"Some secrets are better kept than shared," he insisted. "Please tell no one." He held her stare until she agreed.

Eight

After their talk, Gregorie said he wanted to go into the cave. "I've forgotten the glasses you gave me, and my eyes hurt," he said. He made his way past the slender trunks embedded in between the cliff walls.

Gentille followed after him. She came upon her sunglasses on the floor and helped him push the spindly arms behind his ears. Then she patted his head. "Okay, let's go. Do you want your shoes?"

He hesitated. The trunk, only a few feet away, enticed him with the possibility of a quiet afternoon with Maman, Michaelangela, and Guillaume. And more answers. He still didn't know how he'd ended up in this strange place, and getting into the trunk seemed like the best way to find out.

"It's a beautiful day," Gentille said. "We should go down to the water. Some fresh air will do you good." When he didn't answer, she said, "You know, maybe your desire for blood is just an iron deficiency and not about vampires at all. You've been cooped up in that box for too long."

She frowned in the direction of the trunk as Gregorie

remembered what Paul had said about his unseemly appearance, and how his saying so had made Gentille angry.

"I do not look well?" Gregorie said.

She'd found his shoes and dropped them at his feet, then scanned his face. "Actually, you have some color in your cheeks, which is more than you did yesterday."

"Where will we go? I don't want people to see me." A sudden swell of desperation raised his voice as he slid his feet into the shoes. "I must get back to my home in Saint-Suliac," he said.

Gentille stopped short in front of the tunnel. "What do you mean? You're not leaving Wodge Island, are you?"

"I must get back to France." All at once he wondered where he could buy *un billet de passage*, a ticket for passage—and why hadn't he thought of it before? But a ticket would mean he needed money. "Yes, I will leave the island. Do you know of a boat I can take?"

"Um," she said as she hooked her hair behind her ears. "I'm not sure. Let's go outside. I always get creeped out in this place. I'm not sure why." She hurried through the passage out, and he followed after.

"Are you saying you want to take a boat to France?" she asked.

"I would like to buy a ticket for passage, but I have no money. If I had a boat—"

"Hold that thought." She grabbed his hand and pulled on his arm as if it were a leash. "I want to show you something."

They'd walked to the base of the sand dune before she asked, "Are you a sailor? Where did you say you lived, again?"

"Saint-Suliac, a fishing village, and, yes, I have sailed before." Though he couldn't point to a specific memory, he felt sure of it. "Where are you taking me?"

"Just a place I go to sometimes. A private place where we can talk."

"The cave is not private?"

"You need fresh air, remember? Not even Liam and Paul know about the place I'm taking you to."

They didn't talk while they climbed the dune and then passed the house where the woman had shouted at him when she found him in her yard. The sun beat down on them, and Gregorie appreciated the dark glasses. Drops of perspiration rolled down Gentille's smooth neck, where a subtle rhythmic pulse caught his attention and tempted him to linger. He averted his eyes, and put it out of his mind. When their grasping hands grew slick, he expected her to let go, but she hung on as if certain he would otherwise run from her.

They came to a footbridge that took them over the remainder of the beach and ended at a gravel path. In the distance, he heard a whoosh and hum: perhaps the thing with the glowing orbs from the other night. He skidded to a stop and crouched low to the ground, tugging Gentille down with him.

She yelped. "What's wrong? Who are we hiding from?"

"I hear something."

He put his index finger up to his lips, signaling for her to be quiet. The thing rolled up on wheels, stopping ten paces away. He pointed at it.

"What? The car, you mean?" she said.

"Cart?"

Using her hand to keep the sun at bay, she gazed at the thing on wheels. "Are you afraid of that Jeep that just parked? That car right there?"

Something moved at a quick speed in the distance. Red. Shiny. Spinning wheels. The thoroughfare must be ahead.

"What is a *Jeep*?" he said.

"Ha, ha." She stood as she laughed. "You had me going for a second."

He stared at her, feeling bewildered.

"What," she said, "you don't have cars in France?"

No, we don't, he thought. The humor escaped him.

She laughed again as she continued down the gravel path and he followed after. "Sometimes I can't tell when you're joking."

A manicured lawn mottled with shadows from a couple of tall, widely spread oaks unfurled before them. Flowers with pastel-colored blossoms splashed color here and there, and bushes with shiny green leaves dotted the spaces alongside the pathway. Large polished rocks with words imprinted upon them pressed up from the ground. *Pierres tombales*, he thought. The nearby white building with its red-and-gold windows and cross on the peak of the roof struck him as familiar.

"Cemetery," he said when the word came to him.

"Isn't it beautiful? No one's ever here. It's like my own private park."

A memory barged into Gregorie's mind then: a picnic with Maman. Sunshine, laughter, bread and cheese . . . and Michaelangela, though her blank countenance clued him into her disgruntled feelings: she did not wish to be there.

"Do the graves bother you?" Gentille asked.

"I am an angel of death," he said, "so no, but my friend Michaelangela does not like the cemetery. When she dies, she does not want to be put underground, and she can't understand why anyone would have a picnic in such a place. She once told me," he said, as the memory manifested in greater detail, "that she wishes to be buried at sea."

"I guess she really likes water."

"She loves it," he said, remembering days at the beach, splashing and shouting, and laughing together, just the two of them.

"If you want, we can have a picnic here," Gentille said. "Next time we'll bring food—or *I* will . . . just for me, I guess."

"Maman and I used to picnic in a place very much like this."

The sea breeze made chimes of the leaves overhead, and birds chirped from high branches.

"Good, then you won't think I'm strange when I tell you this is one of my favorite places. I come here by myself all the time. Just to be alone. Just to lie back and listen to the songbirds," she said. "When I first ran away, I hid here—and before I met Liam, I slept here too. If it rained, I ran into the church. If you lie down on a pew in the middle of the nave, the minister won't find you."

"I can see why you would come here," he said, though he didn't find it as inviting as a cave or a trunk to climb into.

She led him to an area thick with overgrown grass and tangled weeds, where no paths crossed and graves had not yet been dug. There she sat, gesturing for him to do the same. She pulled a package of crackers from her pocket and offered it to him. He declined, having no hunger for food.

"Tell me about France and Maman," she said.

He smiled at the thought. "Maman is a healer. The only one in the village."

"Like a doctor, you mean?"

"A healer," he said again. "We work together." He remembered afternoons spent in the woods, searching for various plants, fungi, and stones, and then bringing everything home and making mixtures and poultices with what they had found.

"She must miss you."

"*Oui*. I have to go back. I'm worried about her. Something has happened, something I don't remember. I have a bad feeling when I think of her."

Gentille's happiness seemed to dissipate, some solemn preoccupation taking its place. "I'll miss you when you go. Please don't tell me it will be soon."

"Paul said your family lives on this island," he said. "Don't you want to see them?"

She grasped a handful of grass and ripped it out of the ground. The violent sound of roots snapping filled the air. "I don't want to, and I can't." She grabbed another handful, her sharp eyes daring him to tell her otherwise.

"Where is your mother?" he asked.

"She's at home with my brother and father," Gentille said in a dead tone. "And she's no better off than I was. I chose to leave, but she won't. Believe me, I tried. I wanted the three of us to leave together." She pulled another clump of grass, root ball and all, and tossed it at a nearby tree.

"You, your mother, and your brother?"

"No. God, no," she said as if the question startled her. "I meant the two of us. Can we talk about something else, please?" She stretched her arms behind her back and planted her palms on the ground, propping herself at an angle as tree-mottled rays of the sun dappled her face.

"I'm sorry to make you angry," he said, aware that he had struck a nerve. "I won't tell you to go home."

"Thank you. That's more than most people can manage."

"Do you like living in that yellow thing?"

"The bus? It's not as bad as it seems." A fleeting smile passed over her lips. "I like having my own life. I like being safe."

"I like being safe too. You were not safe at home?" he said. "I'm sorry someone hurt you."

She raised her chin and said, "I'm better off on my own."

He sensed there was something she couldn't get herself to share. She sighed and said, "Why did you leave home?"

"I don't know. I haven't remembered yet."

She put a cracker in her mouth and chewed.

He enjoyed watching her. There was something familiar about everything she did. Even the way she ate a cracker. She was so much like Michaelangela, not only her mannerisms but her looks, the way she smiled and spoke.

"I found my shell, and I am happy about that," he said, "but I have to go to France. Would you like to come to France with me?"

Her jaw went slack, and he saw straight into her mouth to the chewed cracker. She blinked rapidly, as if shocked by a flash of light.

Gregorie continued, "You remind me very much of my neighbor Michaelangela. And you could live with Maman and me. Maman would like you because you are kind."

"Are you serious?" Gentille's hopefulness beamed through her pores.

He could practically feel her longing latch on like hooked fingers intent on keeping him tethered. He sensed admiration and excitement expanding within her chest, a desire to hold him and embrace him—believe in him—as if going to France could be the answer she yearned for.

"I would love that," she said in breathy held-back words. "I'd love to go to France with you. France would be a frickin' dream come true." She took his hand cupped within both of hers, and drew him in. "I'm so glad I met you."

He sensed the warmth gathering inside her body, and along its edges, a faint glow appeared. Her soul, gentle as the light of a quivering candle, was a pure sparkling gold hue that warmed his own.

"Me too," he said.

Then she observed their hands; hers on the outside covered his on the inside. She let go. "You always feel so cold."

While the words were kind, they emerged tinged with suspicion, and he didn't know how to respond, so he just said, "*Oui.*"

Talking about home had made him want to get back to the shell, to remember the past, to see Maman and Saint-

Suliac, Michaelangela and Guillaume and the wood shop once again.

But Gentille had questions about when they would leave and how and where they might get the money they would need, and he didn't have the answers.

And then she stopped talking all at once and stared at the treetops as if an important thought had just arrived: "My family has a boat," she said.

"Your family has a boat?" he echoed. "*Ta famille a un bâteau!*"

Nine

He told her he would like to go back to the cave after that, and she said she'd walk with him because she wanted to go down to the water and put her feet in. They arrived at the cave's entrance when someone called, "Yo! Where've you two love birds been?"

Gregorie recognized Paul's gruff voice.

Gentille spun around and waved. Gregorie did not.

"Hey, guys," Liam said, "we're going to watch the schooner parade. Care to join?"

Gentille clapped and rose up and down on her toes, as if too excited to remain grounded. "Oh, it's fun, Gregorie. You have to see. They have all of these old tall ships on the water, and when the sun goes down, they sparkle with twinkling lights. You'll love it." Then she turned to Liam and Paul and said, "Gregorie lived by the sea in France."

Paul came up behind her and squeezed her waist. "Sounds so romantic when you describe the boat parade like that."

She whirled around and punched him in the chest, the contact occurring with a thud.

Paul exhaled a deep-throated *ugh* and said, "Did you really just *punch* me?"

She groaned and said she was sorry. "It was a reflex. But *I wish you'd stop being such a dick.*" Her voice flared, powered by anger and impatience.

"I just want to know where you've been," he said with alarming seriousness. "I was worried. You know you're like a little sister to me."

"Don't say that, Paul. I told you *never* to say that." She jabbed her finger in his direction. "I am *nobody's* little sister."

Liam didn't pay any attention to them. "So, you want to come with us, Gregorie?"

"Of course he does," Gentille said, her niceness returning when she spoke to Liam.

"I promise you'll love it." She grabbed Gregorie's hand before he could so much as accept the invitation. He'd go because she wanted him to. The shell would have to wait.

Paul stared at Gregorie as Gentille pulled him past. "You look better," he said, scanning him from head to toe. "What'd ya do? Put on a few pounds overnight?"

Gregorie didn't know what to say and wondered why Paul took such an interest in him. He really wished he wouldn't.

"He's been resting," Gentille said. "And recuperating, right, Gregorie?"

Paul scowled. "Jesus, Benicia, it was meant as a compliment. What are you, now, his watchdog?"

She glared in his direction.

"Guys, guys," Liam said, "please stop. I can't take the bickering."

They walked up the beach for a while, the sky growing less blue and more gray as the day neared evening. In the distance, a lighthouse occupied a slender peninsula jutting a good bit into the water. The beach was different here. Some large rocks lined up between the wet sand and the dry, and several people had climbed upon them and made themselves comfortable with folded towels. Others sought out higher ground, spreading their blankets in the sand beyond the rocks. Farther up the beach, a few more cliffs rose from the ground like ancient abandoned buildings.

"Come on," Gentille said, waving Gregorie on. "The ships will come from the right-hand side and pass in front of the lighthouse."

Gregorie followed Gentille and Liam onto one of the boulders. It was flat across its top and smooth and gray for the most part. Still warm from the heat of the day.

Paul did not sit with them. He'd found someone to toss a shiny blue disk back and forth with.

The first ship to come into view captured Gregorie's attention and wouldn't let go. He knew this ship. Or one like it. He imagined ropes in his hands, sea spray, a telescope for seeing long distance. He *must* be a sailor. He hoped he would remember more. Gentille said her family had a boat. Maybe they could sail it to France after all.

Another boat appeared behind the first, and Gregorie began to feel less excited and more ill at ease. Something was not right.

Paul's wicked laugh startled him. Gregorie hadn't noticed him there at the base of the boulder, staring up. "What's the matter, you see a ghost or something? You're, like, so white you're green right now."

Gregorie pointed at the tall ship. "I have seen that boat before. At my home in Saint-Suliac. I believe I have been on that boat."

"San Sooly-what?" Paul said.

"Saint-Suliac, the village I am from."

"Figures," Paul muttered. "Strange guy has to come from a strange place."

What is strange about it? Gregorie wondered.

"I'm gonna have to google that next time I go to the library to charge the phone," Paul said.

"*Google*?" Gregorie asked. "What do you mean *google*? *That* is strange!"

At that, all three of the friends laughed and said he was hilarious.

"You like being mysterious," Paul said. "It's cool." He turned and ran, shouting, "Yo, over here," to the guy who held the blue disk.

The sun dropped below the horizon, and the colors in the sky flared red and orange. The clouds took on a singed and scary shade, stoking the flames of Gregorie's rising bad feelings. The wind picked up, and suddenly the answer to why he was on the ship came to him: *Maman was sick.*

The realization hit him like a flu. Nausea spread from his gut, and a swell of fever filled his head. The terrible urge to return to France swallowed him whole.

The others continued to stare out to sea. Paul took a seat on the stone beside Liam and drank from a can someone had given him. Gentille threw back her head and let the wind tussle her hair, the bangles in her ears rocking to and fro.

Gregorie stifled the urge to leap from the rock and make a run for it. His throat constricted and the result was a small coughing sound that drew Gentille's attention.

"Gregorie, what's wrong?"

"Maman is sick," he said, hoping he didn't sound as desperate as he felt. "I just remembered. I have to go. I have to find out what happened."

"What's he blabbin' about?" Paul said.

"How do you know she's sick?" Gentille asked. "You haven't seen her—"

"I remembered when I saw the ships." He pointed out to sea.

"Well, when did she get sick?"

"I don't know." He hopped to the ground and began pacing back and forth, tamping his urge to run.

"How long have you been away from home?" she asked.

"*Je ne sais pas*. I have to go. I'm sorry!" He waited for her permission.

"But you've only been here a few days," Gentille said, climbing down from the boulder to join him. "You can't have been away that long."

"Okay." He wanted to believe she was right, but something told him *non*.

Paul shouted, "Just let him go. He probably needs to get back to his coffin—or, sorry, I mean his shell. Whatever he calls it."

"Ignore Paul," she told Gregorie. "Do you remember her phone number?"

"*Non*, I don't remember any numbers. If she has numbers, I don't know what they are."

He doubled over, and Gentille placed her hand on his back. "Hey. It's all right," she said.

Slowly he raised his head and gave her his attention.

"You're all right. No matter what's happened," she said. "You're okay."

His head felt stuffed, full of steam. But seeing how much Gentille cared helped.

She patted his back. "You're not alone."

He sensed that someone in her past had said the same to her.

But alone or not alone wasn't his problem. He needed to cross the ocean. He needed to get on a boat and travel back home. He wanted to leave right away, and he would have if he knew where the nearest port was. If he had some money with which to purchase passage.

The darkness and quiet of his shell called to him. It would provide the answers.

“My shell,” he told her, “I need to get back to the cave.”

Her shoulders drooped, and she nodded with surrender. “Okay. I’ll check on you tomorrow, if that’s all right.”

Gregorie started away, walking backward because he didn’t want Gentille to be offended.

Paul raised his hand. “Good-bye and good riddance,” he said.

Liam waved. “Hope you feel better.”

As soon as Gentille began to climb back up the rock, Gregorie turned and ran. He couldn’t reach the cave fast enough, and as he blew through the slender trees and their leafy vines that rattled in his wake, he imagined how good it was going to feel to close himself inside the trunk and remember.

Ten

The Year 1724: Saint-Suliac, France

A little bulging lump peered out of Maman's side. Safely concealed underneath her right arm, it protruded hardly at all. During this time, she began to ingest the turkey tail mushroom and rub salves she'd concocted upon it.

Gregorie sometimes woke in the middle of the night to the sound of her eerie, uttering chants. At twenty-six, he was no longer a boy, and yet her chants sounded powerful and mysterious, and for this reason, they frightened him. He prayed they would work.

They would work, he promised himself.

And yet the lump continued to grow.

Along with it came Maman's lack of appetite, loss of weight, growing weariness, powder-white complexion, and violet swells below her eyes.

Still, she continued to work at Madame Seamstress's and

to heed the call of sick neighbors as well. In the evenings, she pored over Papi's ancient volumes, which she had stowed under her bed for as long as Gregorie could remember. Mystical in nature, these books were not to be toyed with, and she had yet to invite him for a look.

She sat in the armchair in front of the fire, the tomes smearing dust across her lap. Gregorie remembered one night in particular, when she closed the book with a thud and let out a weighty sigh. She called him in from *la cuisine* where he prepared their dinner of bread, cheese, and roasted *legumes.*

"Come sit beside me," she said, "*mon fils.*"

He removed the bread from the oven and placed it upon the cutting board, reluctant to join Maman on the couch because he feared what she would say. He did not want her to die. He had already lost Michaelangela and did not want to lose her too.

Her lips produced a spent smile, evidence of her debilitating energy. "You are no longer a child who needs his mother," she began.

This caused his heart to sink in his chest. "What do you mean? I'll always need you."

"Twenty-six is old enough to live without a mother. But that is not what I want to talk about tonight." She grimaced as she adjusted her position in the chair. "I need you to do something for me."

"*Oui*, whatever it is," he said, ready to leap into action.

"There is a tree in the West Indies. It is called '*la graviola.*' I found it in several of your grandfather's books. I need the leaves and the fruit."

He sensed her desperation to an unsettling degree. "It is a cure?"

The whole of her oozed hopefulness as she closed her trembling eyelids and lowered her chin in a nod.

"Where will I get it?" he said.

"You must go to the jungle and find a healer who can take you to it."

He would drop everything and pack his things. "Is there enough time?"

"Perhaps, if you get on the next ship bound for the West Indies." She placed the book on the floor, then used her arms to push herself to a stand. With a slight falter in her step, she moved across the room to the bookshelf. A clay vase decorated a space in between the books. Turning the vase over, a small cluster of coins fell upon the table. She reached her fingers inside and came out with a wad of folded bills. "Buy a ticket for the next ship that sails. However long it takes will have to be quickly enough."

"Yes, Maman, I'll make the arrangements tonight." He grabbed his jacket and put it on. Then he kissed her cheek before approaching the door.

"Stop by Guillaume's workshop and see if he needs anything in town before you leave," she called after him. "Beatrice has not been well. Perhaps they would like some fresh bread."

"Of course," Gregorie said.

Ever since Michaelangela mysteriously disappeared, Guillaume spent most days and nights in his workshop. It had been nine years since Gregorie had seen Michaelangela's face, heard her laughter, held her hand. She'd been so happy the night they celebrated her seventeenth birthday. Together Gregorie and Maman had selected a special gift for her. A ring with a filigreed silver base and the darkest, densest black stone Gregorie had ever seen. Maman said it was called "obsidian," a word that sounded ominous and powerful, and made Michaelangela smile when she spoke it out loud. It was as stunning as she was, and when she slipped it upon her finger, she said that it made her feel like an adult.

He remembered how badly Michaelangela wanted to be

an adult so she could get away from her overbearing mother—and because she claimed Saint-Suliac bored her. Because she tired of the ocean and the sea air and sunshine, she and Gregorie had already made plans to move away. In just one more year, when they both turned eighteen, they would leave the village together. They would marry and start a new life in another part of France, not too far because he wanted to remain close to Maman, and Michaelangela still wanted to see Guillaume. They had hoped to buy some farmland in one of the larger villages and told no one of their plans.

But then, the morning after Michaelangela's seventeenth birthday, Gregorie woke up and found her gone.

And now, when he arrived at Guillaume's workshop, the door hung open and lamplight spilled into the backyard.

"Come in, come in," Guillaume said, not quite smiling because he no longer smiled easily. "You look like a man with a mission."

"I'm going to the harbor. Do you need anything? Bread, cheese?"

"No," Guillaume said, shaking his head. "I need nothing."

Once a large, cheerful man, Guillaume now appeared sad and shrunken. His face was no longer round or plump, though his business brought wealthy customers from as far as Paris to buy his beautiful furnishings and cabinetry. Each new customer told their friends about the marvelous *artiste* in Saint-Suliac. Everyone these days wanted to own a Martineau, whether it was a chair, table, or bureau.

His furnishings appealed to so many, he claimed, because all of his despair over his daughter's disappearance went into his work. "There is no real beauty without sorrow," he often said. Guillaume halfheartedly joked that his furniture probably collapsed under the immense weight of his sorrow the second his customers brought it into their home.

A heavy silence thickened the air, and Gregorie grasped for

something to talk about. "How is your table coming along?" he finally asked.

"I finished it two days ago and stained it yesterday," he said, gesturing for Gregorie to follow him into the corner of the workshop. The table boasted turned legs of exquisite, grooved detail and a surface as smooth as ice.

As soon as Gregorie saw it, he choked, staggering in response to its beauty. The table gleamed deep brown-red, the color of a human heart. "What kind of wood did you say you used?" he asked.

"Acadia, a fine specimen, the finest I've ever seen," Guillaume said solemnly. "Did you know Michaelangela's middle name is Acadia?"

Gregorie had known. As he continued to gaze at the piece, an overwhelming amount of emotion rose and crested inside of him. "It's unearthly," he whispered.

Guillaume stared at the ground. "So was my child."

A familiar, lifeless veil of downheartedness crossed Guillaume's face, and silence settled over the wood shop once again while Gregorie attempted to revive his own optimism.

When Michaelangela's search party had turned up empty-handed, Gregorie had vowed to find her himself. With no trail to set him in the right direction—not one clue to point him any particular way—he had traveled by horse, visiting every town they'd ever dreamed of possibly inhabiting once matrimony had bound them. But no one had seen the girl he described, the one who'd quite possibly left home with only the white dress on her back and the stone of obsidian on her finger.

Weeks later, he returned home, defeated, praying she would come back on her own. Years later, he was still hoping she would.

"She's not gone forever," Gregorie said, wanting to believe it himself.

"I think that she is," Guillaume said with resign. "I *feel* that she is."

"I'm still going to find her one day," he said.

"You already tried that. Perhaps she doesn't want to be found. What if leaving was her plan all along?"

"If that were so, she would have told me. We were—"

"I know. You were going to be married. You were always very close," Guillaume said, placing a hand on Gregorie's shoulder. "No one disputes that. But she and her mother . . . " He stopped, clasped his hands together. "As we both know, Michaelangela often threatened—no, not even threatened—she *promised* to leave. My daughter had an independent streak as wide as a canyon. I swear, sometimes I could see a fire burning within her."

Gregorie nodded, fighting the urge to defend her. "She wouldn't leave without me, so something must have happened," he said. "Someone must have—" He skidded to a halt, regretting his words. They both knew that if she didn't leave because she wanted to, it meant someone had taken her against her will. If someone had taken her, it was not for good reason.

"I'm sorry," Gregorie said. "What I meant to say is that there must be an explanation."

"Maybe so," Guillaume agreed. "If that's what you believe, I will hold on to my last shred of hope for her return. I know how much you loved her," he said.

"Yes, hold on to it," Gregorie said. "Please hold on to it as long as you can."

They stood in silence, observing the table together.

"Why are you going to the harbor this evening?" Guillaume asked.

"I must book passage to the West Indies. Maman needs something special to help her heal."

"How is she doing?"

"*Bon*," Gregorie said, though he also shook his head, a subconscious gesture because what he said wasn't true. "I must go."

Guillaume lifted a polishing cloth from the shelf and pressed it to the tabletop. "*Bonne chance, mon ami*. I truly hope you find what you're looking for."

Gregorie tried to smile when he said, "*Merci*."

Eleven

Rousing from the memories of his life in Saint-Suliac, Gregorie emerged from the trunk prepared to book passage to France. He had one foot in the box and one out when he realized Gentille stood there, only a few steps away in the cave's mottled light, watching and waiting.

"How long have you been—"

"Ten minutes," she said. "I wanted to make sure you were all right, after the way you left last night."

"Oh yes, I'm all right. Maman is sick. I remembered when I saw the ships, and I needed to remember more so I hurried back here."

"Uh-huh," she said with nervous bobs of her head. "And, I also wanted to ask you if you meant what you said. About me coming to France with you."

He glanced upward to the top of the cave and observed the dusty sunlight streaming in. "It is morning?"

"Yes."

"Good. We must make a plan."

"Paul said he doubted you were going to France," she said

slowly, "and that even if you were, you wouldn't take me with you."

Gregorie's brow crumbled into question. "Why would Paul say such a thing? I *do* want you to come." He closed the trunk and sat on top of it.

She let out a held breath and said, "Thank goodness, because now I have my heart set on it. I think moving to France could work out really well for—"

"Come sit beside me," he said. "We will make a plan. You have a boat."

"My family does. It can get us off the island."

"Off the island," he said, "but not to France."

She laughed. "No. Not to France. We're going to have to find another way."

This was bad news. "So, then, where do the tall ships take harbor?"

"You mean the ships we saw last night? I'm not sure." Shoulders shrugging, she appeared to have entered a befuddled state.

"We need to book passage."

"Right," she said, "but I don't think those are the ships that sail to France. And if we are going to book passage, we also need money."

"I have no francs."

"Not even an account at home?"

"*Aucune*. I own nothing. Except for my shell. That is all."

"Okay," she said with some hesitation. "Well, I've got a bank account, but there's only a couple hundred in it, and my debit card is on the mainland with my passport, in a locker at the Point Jeremiah ferry station."

"Your debit card?"

"You know, my money," she said. "It's like a credit card, only you don't owe the money. The money is already yours. But you can actually use it as a credit card if you need more."

He blinked. Their conversation was growing more and more confusing as time passed. "So, your money is on the mainland?"

It seemed a simple question, but the way she rubbed her face and then looked away made him wonder.

"I know that's weird," she said. "I was going to leave the island at one point, in a moment of panic, but I changed my mind."

He didn't quite understand. "What happened?"

She shook her head, her cheeks flushing. "I couldn't do it. I couldn't leave."

They exchanged a weighty glance, and he knew she wouldn't tell him more.

"Anyway," she continued, "we can use the card if it's not expired." She paused. "The problem is that at the moment we have no money for the ferry to take us to Point Jeremiah and the locker."

"We will take your family's boat to the mainland," Gregorie said, "and then we must find a way to purchase our tickets to board the ship that will take us to France."

"Are you set on taking a boat—we might be better off flying."

"Flying? Yes, with the birds," he said with a chuckle. "*Très amusante.*"

"On a plane. You've never flown, I take it?" She pointed at the cave's ceiling.

When he realized she meant what she said, a spasm of fear coursed through his body. *What kind of place is this?* he wondered.

She said nothing.

"There is a way to fly?" he said.

"It'll cost less than a cruise liner will, I'm sure. Maybe that's what we should do. We'll cross the bay in my boat and take a cab to the airport. We'll charge my card. If it hasn't expired."

"Expired."

She huffed out her exasperation. "I may have the money for the tickets to get us to France, is what I'm saying. But I don't know for sure."

"Okay, okay, so we need the family boat to get to the mainland." That's as far as Gregorie's brain would take him for the moment. The rest he'd figure out as they went along. "How do we get it?"

"I'll have to sneak into my parents' house and steal the keys. I know exactly where my father keeps them. The boat is at the marina, of course."

"And this will be easy to do?" he asked.

"It shouldn't be too hard," she said with determination. "But when we're done with the boat, someone has to get it and bring it back to the marina. Liam can do it, if he can get the money for the ferry. He and Paul will have to go down to the public beach with empty coffee cups and see what they can scrape together. It's not like they haven't done it before. The only thing I'm really worried about is the Coast Guard stopping him."

"What will the guard do?"

"They'll throw him in a cell and tell my parents the boat has been stolen, and then my brother will probably come after him. Either way, he'll be charged with theft."

"*Non*, that cannot happen. We will simply leave the boat at the mainland."

"At the ferry station?"

"Yes, there."

"Oh my gosh, yes. We'll park the boat and abandon it. Someone will eventually notice when no one comes for it, and they'll check the registration stickers. It won't be long before they return it to my parents."

"Right. The stickers," he said, no idea what *stickers* were but liking the enthusiastic way Gentille had responded to his plan.

"This could work," she said. "I'm so glad we figured this out."

He stood and pulled up his pants, retying the string because it always loosened. "Oui, let's go."

She didn't stand. She remained just as she was with her gaze fixed on him.

"What?"

"I'm just wondering. Are you hungry at all?"

"No. Not at all," he said with ease because it was true. He was never hungry.

"I'm just wondering when you might need another drink."

She meant the blood.

"Hopefully never," he said more confidently than he felt. He didn't want her to fear him because he didn't want her blood. He didn't want blood at all, except for the two times when the need had come on like a sudden storm. "Maybe I'm cured."

"That would be nice," she said, "but do you think it's possible?"

"Everything is possible," he said, and he wanted to believe it.

OUTSIDE, dark clouds gathered low on the horizon above the sea.

"A storm is coming?" he asked, shifting the sunglasses on top of his head so he could judge the color of the sky.

"I've seen gray clouds hovering out there a million times, and they never turn in. Don't worry. It's a beautiful day."

He nudged the glasses back onto his nose.

They walked the beach. Past the place where he had come ashore. Past a stretch of sand crowded with people in colored under things. Past a road with many moving cars and unlit orbs. After a time, he and Gentille climbed a hill of sand, left the beach, and followed a walking path where they came upon a row of skinny wheeled things (much smaller than cars) with metal frames and black cushions. Gentille called them "bicycles" and pulled one from the rack. He checked around to see if anyone was watching them.

"Go ahead, take one. We're allowed. They're just lenders. We can borrow one here and ride it to a rack across town. They're all over Wodge Island."

"We are not stealing?"

"No, we're merely borrowing, and it's allowed. Have you ever ridden a bicycle?"

He shook his head. "We don't have them in Saint-Suliac."

This world was strange, and Saint-Suliac was normal, and frankly, he couldn't wait to get back to France.

"If you don't know how, we'll have to double. I'll pedal, and you can sit." Then she said, "Don't worry, you don't weigh much. I'll be fine."

She held the thing by its metal bars. He came up behind her and hesitated, not knowing what she wanted him to do.

"Like this," she said after a few seconds. "Put your leg over and sit on the seat. I'll stand on the pedals. Don't worry, I'm stronger than you think. I've pedaled Liam before."

"You can do this in your skirt?" he said.

She flashed him a frown. "Don't be sexist."

He did as she told him, no idea what *sexist* was and still nervous about the prospect of falling off the thing's strangely shaped seat.

She struggled to get the wheels moving, towing him and the bike together. As she pedaled, though, it became easier. He held her bare, brown waist and felt the air caressing his face and the sun singeing his skin the way it did whenever it touched him unhindered. She pedaled for a few more minutes, until they came to an ascending hill. There, she put her feet down, held the bike by its front bars, and waited for him to get off.

Her cheeks were red and her forehead glistened. She was out of breath.

"I don't breathe hard like you do," he said as he dismounted.

She made an angry, curt laugh. "Are you saying I'm out of shape?"

"I mean, I don't breathe," he said. "Not anymore. I used to."

Her annoyance fell away, and the kindness returned to her face. "You probably just don't notice you're doing it."

"*Non*, I actually don't do it at all."

"Oh," she said softly and then she grew silent for a moment.

"We need to go one block that way," she pointed to the left. "I'll hop the fence into the neighbor's yard and check the garage to see if anyone's home."

"They will be in the garage?"

"No," she said, with a little laugh that ended in a snort. "The *cars* will be there. But my parents should be at the club at this hour, having breakfast."

Why in the world they'd need one of those noisy, scary things, he didn't know. Especially when the town provided these bicycles.

"You do realize that most people *have* cars, don't you Gregorie," she said bluntly. "Why don't you know this?"

"*You* don't have one," he said. "Liam and Paul don't have one."

She shook her head. "We'll talk about this later. I have to

concentrate on what I'm doing right now. My brother might be home, but he'll be sleeping. Lazy shit never gets up before noon unless the phone wakes him."

"Tell me the truth," Gregorie said, grasping her hand. "Is this safe for you to do?"

"Don't worry. I can outrun them if they happen to catch me in the act. My father's knees are shot, and my mother never wears anything but four-inch heels. Just stay here, with the bike. I'll be back in a few minutes."

As she climbed the fence, Gregorie worried her skirt would catch on the tips of the wooden spikes, but she made it over easily, as if she'd done this many times before. A hole left by a knot in the wood allowed him to watch her as she moved in a crouched position toward a cluster of bushes in the yard. A rope swing hung from one of the bigger trees—he'd seen swings before—and a bench and pools of flowers decorated the rest. A doll lay sprawled on the ground, like a little girl who'd been forgotten.

Gentille climbed a staircase to a wooden platform and instead of going straight to the door, she walked over to some potted plants and tipped one sideways. She hurried to the back door and unlocked it. Once she entered the house, he lost sight of her.

He waited, resting against the fence with the bicycle leaned upon its skinny metal leg, worrying vaguely that it might start to roll away. He hummed a tune that came to him without effort, remembering the words as if they rode a stream that flowed through his mind: *Au clair de la lune, Mon ami Pierrot, Prête-moi ta plume, pour écrire un mot, Ma chandelle est morte, Je n'ai plus de feu. Ouvre-moi ta porte, pour l'amour de dieu*. Then a car chugged past—he'd never get used to those things—and something came over the fence and landed with a slap upon the concrete beside him. "*Mon dieu*," he cried before realizing it was just Gentille returning.

He laughed a little before noticing the redness around her eyes, as if she'd been rubbing them. "What happened? Did they try to stop you?"

She sobbed into her hand for a moment before sniffing loudly and shaking her head. "No. I got the key to the boat. I was just . . . scared."

"You are brave," he told her, and she grabbed him with both arms and pressed her face into his shoulder. Gregorie couldn't imagine why she was crying when everything had worked out as planned. "Leaving is not what you want? Maybe you shouldn't go," he said, remembering Michaelangela and how she may have left her home on purpose—and then may have regretted it.

"No. It *is* what I want."

"I understand. Even if it is what you want, you are still sad to leave them."

"It's just . . . " She stopped talking and wiped her cheeks with the bottom of her skirt.

He waited for her answer.

"It's complicated. We need to go." She took the bike's handlebars in her hands and gestured for him to get on.

"Okay, I am ready." He swung his leg over. Just as she got into position to take off, he asked, "Do you have a little sister?"

She said nothing at first, and then, "Why do you ask?"

"I saw a doll in the yard."

"Oh. No. No sisters. It must be the neighbor's or something. Are you ready? Downhill will be much faster, so hold on."

THEY BUMPED and wobbled at times, and coasted at others. Gentille had to pedal a long time before they reached the avenue that led to the boatyard.

Straight ahead, in the near distance, the clouds loomed fat, gray, and devious.

"It's going to storm?" Gregorie said, not sure she had noticed.

"Maybe," she said, gazing upward. "But we need to do this. It's probably just going to drizzle."

"Are you certain?" The clouds appeared angry to him. The kind that buzzed with lightning. And wind. "Maybe we should go another day."

"It's fine," she said with finality.

They approached the gated entrance to the harbor. "Just pretend you belong here, like you've been here a million times," she told him. "It's my family's boat, so technically I'm not stealing. And the guys who work here should recognize me."

"We are only borrowing," Gregorie said.

"Right."

"Will you know the way to the mainland?"

"Yes, of course. Don't worry. I know what I'm doing. We'll get the boat, and then we'll stop on the other side of the island to say goodbye to Liam and Paul, and then—"

"My shell!" Gregorie yelped. He'd almost forgotten about it, and now that he had remembered, his nerves flew into a panic. "I can't go without my shell, Gentille!"

"Okay, okay, calm down. We'll go back for the shell. Just don't shout like that again. You scared the crap out of me."

At the end of the marina's driveway, they came to one of the racks with the lender bicycles and dismounted. Walking down a gray, weather-worn deck, they hurried past a wooden house with white trim. It was lit up on the inside, the front window filled with shirts, fishing poles, boots, and things he didn't recognize.

"That's where the marina guys work," Gentille said as she waved to the two young men inside. One of them waved back, then hopped off his chair and approached the front door, a bell jangling as he opened it and leaned out.

"Keep walking," she told Gregorie.

The guy shouted, "There's a storm coming our way. 'Bout ten minutes out."

"We're just taking a short trip," Gentille said with ease. "No more than a few minutes. I need to check on one of my traps."

"Make it quick. Supposed to be a rough one."

"K, thanks!" she said, overly cheerful as she jogged to catch up to Gregorie.

They were halfway down the dock, passing many slips when the terrible need struck him. A delicious, disgusting scent riding a wind gust tapped into some wild, driving force within him, and at once he lost the battle to deny it. He took a sharp left turn toward the aroma, with Gentille's "Where are you going?" a mere mosquito buzz in his ear.

The dock broke left as well, and he reached a ramp that led downward. Instead of running across it, he took a flying leap from the upper dock to the lower and came upon a shiny white box with red, watery liquid puddled inside.

"Wait, Gregorie, don't—" Gentille shouted in an alarmed voice he'd never heard her use before.

But he couldn't stop himself. His desire for the blood barged through him like water plummeting over the side of a cliff. He dove at the box and slurped up all the liquid to be had, both inside and that which had spilled upon the deck boards.

When it was gone, he withstood a horrible case of embarrassment. He had acted like a starved pig at a trough. And yet the blood pulsing through him provided great gushing pleasure. Forgetting his remorse, his eyelids came down and he allowed himself a moment to indulge in the warm, satisfying waves of euphoria.

When he opened them, he didn't know how much time had passed. Gentille stood at the top of the ramp, gaping at him, her back hunched and jaw tense with concern. She seemed to be hovering in a moment of indecision, unsure of whether to fly off or stay put.

He hurried toward her, bright new energy surging in his limbs. Instead of climbing the ramp, he took it in one leap and landed in front of her.

This caused her to gasp and jump back. She braced herself as if ready for a fight.

He bowed his head and straightened his arms at his sides. "I'm so sorry. I couldn't stop. But I'm okay now. I promise. We must go."

Her shoulders slumped, and she tilted her head. What he'd done seemed to have whisked away all of her energy and excitement for their plan. "How long has it been since the last time you drank?"

He eased back on his heels, shame poisoning the wonderful feelings. "I don't know. It won't happen again for at least a few days, I promise. You can trust me. You can."

She cringed. "I can smell it on you. The blood. And it was *yesterday*, when I saw you in that woman's backyard," she said, her voice growing harsh. She grabbed her forehead and groaned. "What am I doing? What the hell was I thinking?"

"*Non, non*, don't say that," he begged her. "I *can* promise. I will make sure it doesn't happen. I'll figure out a way to—"

"Not need blood in order to survive?"

"Yes. Or, uh, *non*." He knew he couldn't make that promise though she needed him to make it. He would promise anyway. "I can drink fish blood. You just saw me do it. Or deer blood. Meat juices."

Either way, Gentille was his friend, and she was not in danger. There was no reason their plan for France couldn't work. "Come, we have to go. We have only a few minutes before the storm, and we will figure this out later." He pointed at the darkening sky.

The wind whipped strands of hair across her face as she scanned the horizon.

"You're right," she said, without the fervor she'd displayed earlier. "The guys in the marina shop saw us. If we don't take the boat now, they might tell my father—or my brother—that they saw us here."

He grabbed her shoulders with both hands and squeezed gently as he peered into her eyes, longing to make that deeper connection he often felt with her. "You have your heart set on France? You still want to go?"

She said nothing but nodded weakly, then continued down the main dock, passing boats to either side. Gentille hopped into the one with "Second Wind" written on the back. Right away, she began to work, leaping on the boat and off, untying this rope and knotting that one, inserting the key in its place at the boat's helm.

It wasn't the type of ship Gregorie had been expecting: a tall ship like one he'd sailed on from France. It was small and had no sails. Which was odd. Like the others parked in the marina, a boulder of a thing attached to the back. He didn't know what to do, how to prepare or help, so he stayed out of the way and basked in the strange energy the blood had provided him.

If Gentille minded, she didn't show it. She didn't seem to want or need him to do anything.

She turned the key beside the surprisingly small steering wheel, and the vessel roared to life with a loud growling vibration. Frightened, Gregorie dropped into a crouched position, then crawled to the front of the boat to get further from the source of the noise. He climbed into the seat across from Gentille's.

Her nostrils flared, perhaps because she thought him odd. "It's just the motor," she said sternly.

The sky darkened to the color of slate. The air grew heavy, as if something above pressed the canopy of clouds toward the earth. The idea that they should not be doing this crossed his mind, but Gentille continued to ready the boat. It was their one chance, and they had already decided to take it.

"Undo that last rope beside you," she shouted, and as soon as he did, she hopped into the captain's seat and pressed down on a metal arm, causing the motor to chug. Slowly they passed the vessels that remained tied to the docks, the thrum of the motor like a grumbling whale, until they reached a wide open lane and Gentille increased the ship's speed. His hair blew back from his face while cool breezes raced in and out of his nostrils and ears.

Up ahead, fingers of lightning reached down from the clouds like the lighted legs of a giant spider in the sky. They met with the ocean, and soon the rumble of thunder broke.

Gentille bit her bottom lip. "Shit," she said.

A FEW MINUTES IN, the rain came down in buckets. Gentille stayed the course. "Too late to go back," she said. "We have the boat now. We can't risk returning it. We'll have to hide it in one of the coves and spend the night in the bus."

Gregorie did not want to postpone their trip to the mainland. He did not want to spend the night with Paul and Liam, who would now have ample time to talk Gentille out of their plan to leave. Even if leaving was what she wanted, they were her friends and he was new to them. They would be protective.

To top it off, a sudden strong dislike for boats came over him and fear of the water, as if he'd just remembered that he couldn't swim—but he could swim, and this was a good boat, so that didn't make sense.

Gentille lowered their speed as growing waves began to lift and drop them, lift and drop them. Gregorie's knuckles became white from gripping the edges of the seat that held him. Something familiar grew out of this feeling: a memory. His stomach became queasy, and soon the fear of drowning submerged him.

The wind swooped down from the sky, and the waves grew in size. Gregorie worried for his life even though he no longer breathed and no longer ate and might even have been half dead at that point. He needed to get back to Maman, and he couldn't do that if he became lost at sea.

What happened to me? he wondered. *How have I ended up on this strange island?*

He was supposed to travel to the West Indies. He needed to retrieve the plant that would cure Maman. He had booked passage, he knew that much. Something must have occurred on that voyage. Something bad.

Was it a storm like this one? A storm on the high seas?

He felt the answer in his gut, and a horrible, sick wave of terror threatened to break upon his heart.

There *was* a storm. He was a passenger on *Le Chanceux*, a tall ship headed to the West Indies.

As the rain came down and Gentille struggled to stay the course, Gregorie stared out at the roiling, foaming waves . . . and remembered.

Twelve

The Year 1724: Atlantic Ocean

A third member of the crew had turned up dead.

They found this one in the galley. Beside the stove, a pot of green beans overturned at his feet. He'd been drained of blood, just like the two dead men before him.

For this reason, Gregorie stayed in his cabin as much as possible with his cabinmate, a Spanish-speaking boy, younger and skinnier than himself, who every night sipped from a bottle of port and passed out. Rumors amongst the crewmen and passengers spoke of lacerations of the sort a wolf might leave behind—or a snake. *Anaconda*, he'd heard some of the crew say, though Gregorie had read an entire book on snakes and knew for a fact that anaconda didn't use venom to kill.

Sometimes on ships like these, the crew lied, especially if seamen or passengers had died of illness. This he knew because he'd traveled once before, with Maman, when he was very young.

So, whether wolf or snake or plague threatened, Gregorie remained in his cabin. Until he ran out of water or the killer had been caught, he'd stay put. The Spanish boy didn't share whatever nuts and dried fruit he'd brought from home, and, two days before, Gregorie had finished the bread and cheese Maman had sent with him. His stomach growled for an entire day and most of the following night before he decided it would be safe enough to visit the galley and claim the rations he'd foregone. He'd go at midnight. Not many would roam the boat at that hour. And hopefully he wouldn't run into any venomous snakes. Or wolves.

He slipped out of his cabin, groggy from lack of nourishment, and headed for the galley. He didn't know the layout of the boat well and became confused, ending up just outside the captain's cabin. He had a poor sense of direction, so he wasn't surprised that he'd ended up in the wrong place. He came to a ladder and, sensing the coolness of fresh air, climbed up.

After staying indoors for so long, stepping into the night air was like immersing himself in a refreshing pool. So revitalizing and welcome was the feeling, so crisp and clear, that he'd forgotten he'd wanted to avoid all other passengers and crew. He stood there, under the full brightness of the moon, and drank it in.

He was on the stern end, just below the elevated poop deck. On the opposite side of the ship, a sailor leaned against the rail and smoked a cigarette. *Nothing to worry about, just a man having a well-deserved break,* he told himself.

Gregorie breathed deeply. Breathing fresh air felt almost as good as he imagined eating or drinking would. Silver rays splashed across the sea, and he remembered what Maman had said about Papi lighting the moon. After his grandfather had died, his soul passed through the heavens on its way to *la lune.*

That was because he was an angel of death, just like Gregorie was. *It's nice to see you, Papi,* Gregorie thought. Then he noticed a strange haze encircling the moon as if the smoke from a fire had encapsulated it in the midst of a pearl-gray bubble. The thought of fire led him to thoughts of cooking—and hunger. His stomach grumbled, and he decided to give himself just one more minute with Papi before descending the ladder and searching for whatever scraps he might find in the galley.

He whispered *au revoir*, and when he turned toward the ladder, two men stood where before there had only been one. The second man, a large one dressed richly in coat, breeches, and silk stockings, pressed his open mouth to the smoking sailor's neck.

An intimate moment, Gregorie assumed.

Embarrassed by his intrusion, he bowed his head, pretending not to have seen. He would quietly return to the ladder and step down—but then two knee-knocking thuds and a startling clatter stopped him. Someone had slipped and fallen? Or maybe the two men fought? Gregorie stole a glance portside once again. The crewman, now alone, lay on the deck with his arm outstretched in Gregorie's direction.

With great effort and terrible strain, the man rasped a whispery, *Help me.*

Of course Gregorie would help. He and Maman had a talent for healing. When someone was ill, they answered the call. Gregorie ran the length of the boat and dropped to his hands and knees. The man lay on his side. A wound at the neck trickled a steady stream of blood, so Gregorie placed his hand upon it and pressed, the blood turning his fingers red and slippery.

"No," the man said, slapping at Gregorie's upper body. "Don't."

"I must apply pressure," Gregorie insisted, because that is

what Maman would have done when faced with such an injury.

"Let me go." The crewman's chest heaved with his effort to speak.

Gregorie pulled back to observe the man's agitated state before studying the two puncture wounds, inches apart, marring his neck. Could this be the work of a wolf or a snake? And where had the other man gone? Why would he leave his friend in this state? Unless it was the second man who had done this—*the second man who had pressed his mouth to this man's neck!*

The crewman hacked, his lips fast becoming flat and colorless. "He made me drink—" He tried to say more but blood gurgled up his throat, and he spasmed in a coughing fit. "My heart is near to stopping," he rasped. "You must kill me before I begin—"

"I cannot do that, *monsieur*, you know not what you say." Gregorie internally implored the moon, wishing Papi could tell him what to do, knowing what Maman would do, how she would continue to treat the victim as best she could.

But this man would not make it easy. He reached for Gregorie, fumbling around the neck of his shirt, loosely gripping it and then attempting to push Gregorie away. His gaze floated upward, and he fell back, his body going limp. "Put a stake through my heart," he said.

Obviously he was mad. And now Gregorie sensed something strange happening to the man's soul. A pulling and pushing, back-and-forth kind of sinking and rising. A wrestling match of wills, perhaps? He would wait and see if indeed the heart stopped, and if so, he would help to release the soul as best he could.

The blood continued to seep through the gashes at the neck, and the sailor's haggard breathing settled and became slow. His eyelids fainted closed, and his pulse reduced to the meager tap of a second hand. It would only be a moment now.

In the midst of this quiet release, a hissing sound inserted itself into Gregorie's ear like a whisper in a language he'd never heard. It sent a cold shiver up his back that manifested in hunched shoulders and a feeling of paranoia. Was someone watching? Gregorie twisted around to see who or what had made the utterance but found no one. Certainly the killer would not be bold enough to return to the scene of the crime, to risk showing his face. High upon the main mast, a flag shimmied in the wind; perhaps it was the flag that had made the hissing sound.

The man's weakened breaths rasped ever more gently in his throat; the blood no longer spilled from his neck. It was time. Gregorie closed his eyes to better sense the sailor's soul. In his mind, he offered his outstretched hands and waited to see if the soul would grab on. Gregorie had been an angel of death for more than a dozen years. He knew well what needed to be done. It was not as strenuous a task as it had been when he was a boy. All he had to do was settle his mind.

Finally, the man's soul grabbed on, and Gregorie began to pull.

Some souls came through more easily than others. Some clung to their physical form, fearful of what they would find in the afterlife, but soon, with Gregorie's gentle urging, they'd let go. This one required more than the usual effort. It was as if Gregorie were in a tug-of-war with some other force that also wanted the man's soul. But Gregorie was well practiced, and he was not about to let this man become stuck. He concentrated with greater intensity and raised his internal arms, using all of his mind's strength. Like a flower plucked from the earth, the soul broke free.

Gregorie opened his eyes. The first glimmer of light mixed with the crewman's deathly complexion, hovering for a moment, as all souls did, before fully exiting the body. Once free, it became a wisp of a cloud on its own accord, a fuzzy shimmering glow that soon blended with the air and became one with the night.

"Go with grace," Gregorie said, and he sat back, allowing the wall of the ship to support him. He drew a cleansing breath and scanned the deck to make sure no one had seen. It remained deserted, so while he regained his spent strength, he took a moment to revel in the satisfaction of doing a good deed.

Then he remembered that the dead crewman had been murdered, and he stood, leaving the man just as he was when he had passed. The others would find him soon enough. Gregorie wanted to get out of there as quickly as he could, but blood covered much of his hands and forearms.

He hurried to a barrel filled with seawater and began to scrub, but then he sensed a dark presence and a shiver rode the back of his neck. Instinct told him to run, but as soon as he removed his arms from the water and took a step in the direction of the nearest ladder, he knew he was caught.

The large man who'd bitten the sailor blocked his way. Eerily silent and focused, his entrancing gaze harpooned Gregorie in place. His hands, the size of buckets, reached out and snatched Gregorie from the ground he stood on. Before he knew it, the monster of a man had tugged his hair so harshly that his head thrust backward and fully exposed his neck.

A dog barked, and someone shouted, "You! What're you doing there?"

Boots collided with deck boards as men crossed *Le Chanceux*, crying, "Stop right there," and "We've got you now." The dog's hysterical bark continued. In the next breath, Gregorie plummeted backward, no longer supported or held.

The killer was gone.

After that, Gregorie would not leave the cabin. Not for food, water, or air. He didn't care that at least a fortnight of travel lay before him. He would rather starve or suffocate than encounter the monster who'd tried to drink his blood.

His young cabinmate had ventured out two days before, hoping to bring back some food and drink, but had yet to return. To make matters worse, a storm had arrived that morning and the rocking of the vessel grew more severe with every hour. The boat swooned as if it were a pendulum hung from the sun, swooping and lulling to one side and then the other.

Covered with a blanket, Gregorie huddled in his bunk, scared and sick from lack of sustenance.

Still, he would not leave the cabin.

After several days, a forceful knock sounded down the hall. "Anybody in there? We need men to sail the ship." A door opened, then soon slammed shut. Footsteps neared and Gregorie threw off the blanket that covered him and scuttled under his bed, hoping to go unnoticed should whoever it was enter uninvited.

"Where in the name of Mary has everyone gone?" Another door opened, then closed. "Is anyone down here? Anyone at all?"

Gregorie squeezed his eyes closed as if doing so might be enough to take him far from this nightmare of a ship.

The door of his cabin opened, and from his hiding place, he saw a crewman's pants soaked through and through.

"Please, God, there has to be someone on this ship," the crewman said. "I can't be the only one."

Everyone is dead, Gregorie thought. *How can this be?*

He peered out from under the bunk. The person standing before him was indeed a crewman, but not a man. It was a woman, though her shoulders stretched as wide as most men's. "Tell me it's not true," Gregorie said. "The entire crew, all of the passengers? They cannot all be dead."

The woman dropped to her knees and grabbed both of Gregorie's wrists, pulling him to the center of the cabin floor where he stared into her pale, freckled face framed with cropped red hair. "The storm is upon us," she said, "and there isn't anyone to man the ship. Come, you must help me get her out of the fray."

As she stood, she pulled Gregorie to his feet, his legs scrabbling to get underneath him. "But where are the passengers?" he said. "There were over one hundred passengers on this voyage."

Nausea rose up his throat as a possibility dawned on him: Could the monster have thrust back each one of their necks, then tossed their lifeless bodies into the sea?

"Come," the woman said. "If we don't get out of this thing soon, it'll be the end for us and anyone else hidden under their bunk."

Fighting his trembling fear and reluctance, Gregorie followed her up the ladder to the main deck, where gale winds slapped his face as if furious with him for remaining in his cabin for so long. The sea spray burned as he clenched the side of the staggering boat and observed the tattered sails flapping like the wings of exhausted birds.

"Over here," the woman shouted from only a few feet away. He did his best to keep his balance as the ship lurched drastically to one side, then he stumbled toward her and a pair of ropes dangling in the middle of the ship.

With the next ocean swell, he fell into the mast and took it in a hug. "Where is the crew!" he shouted over the howling gale.

The woman merely shook her head. "I'm going to man the helm," she yelled. "All you have to do is make sure the sails aren't destroyed. Hold these," she said, pointing at the two ropes in front of him. "If the wind becomes too much, pull them down."

Once again, Gregorie gazed upward at the sails she referred to—two drenched cloths like the moth-eaten drawers of a giant. All of the others were gone. He didn't know how he was going to hold onto the ropes or be of any help. He worried that if he let go of the mast, his body would spiral away like a dead leaf in the wind.

The woman strode away from him, the rain pelting her viciously as she shielded her face.

Gregorie let go of the mast and grasped the two ropes. The ship leaned into a severe angle, and he tripped over his own feet and fell onto his backside. Still, he held tight to the ropes, his palms burning.

From the floor of the ship, he stared at the great sails and how they'd already been ripped to shreds and knew in his heart that he and this woman had no chance of getting out of the storm alive. They plunged and then climbed with each cresting wave, and Gregorie's fear spun in his chest as he rose to his knees and prayed to Maman. He told her how sorry he was that he would not make it to the West Indies. He knew that for sure. The wind pulled at his soaked hair, and he tipped back his head and begged the dark, moonless sky for mercy. "Papi," he called. "Help me, Papi!"

That's when the unusually large man appeared starboard, the impression of him like a dark shadow. He had set his sights on Gregorie and moved toward him in spite of the rain and the wind that should have slowed him down. No dogs or men would show up to save Gregorie this time. They were dead, and he would be next.

Through the spray of sea and brutal rain, and in spite of the waves crashing overhead, the giant trudged forward while

Gregorie gripped the ropes with the intention of remaining alive.

"I've been waiting for you," the man said, his voice a deep, shivering hiss. He grabbed Gregorie by his hair, and like that, the ropes snapped away, and Gregorie slammed into the wall that was the monster's oversize body. With his head thrown back, a ruthless force impaled his neck.

It happened so fast. The stabbing pain struck like two large needles piercing his flesh. But soon enough the agony receded and the sound of the storm's chaos seemed to have retreated under a blanket of thick cotton, taking with it the whipping wind and the violent creaking of the hull stretched to its limit. A feeling of calm settled in, and the cold siphoned away and left him with a pounding, rushing internal warmth of the sort he'd never experienced before. It wasn't the kind of warmth he enjoyed lying in the arms of Michaelangela. It was an ominous sort of warmth, frightening and helpless, the kind he realized might lead to death. A bright beam of light streamed in behind his eyes. Light like liquid, pooling and blotting away all of the awful reality in front of him: the ship and the storm and the monster intent on draining him of blood. All of these worries disappeared because he could no longer see beyond the illumination to the earthly world.

"That's far enough," the monster said in a gruff voice. "When all of this is through, I'm going to need your help."

With that, the rain and wind and cold returned. Gregorie snapped out of the peaceful, bright place and woke with the horrid man's arm dripping blood in his nostrils, upon his cheeks, close enough to enter his mouth. The tang of metal on his tongue made him gag, and he spat at once.

Then the monster dropped him, and Gregorie fell to his knees and retched.

"Is the taste of my blood so horrible?" the oversize man

said, chuckling with humility. “Ah, but thanks to me, you won’t die.”

The ship dropped into a great careening swell then, as if all of the water in the sea had run out and they would become grounded at its very bottom. The ropes Gregorie had been holding had risen as they never should have and what was left of the sails had dropped to the deck. The captain’s wheel spun frantically as if manned by the ghost of a madman. The woman at the helm was gone, most likely tossed overboard, or maybe she had jumped to save herself from the monster.

The only thing Gregorie knew at that moment was that he and the blood-sucking giant would both go down with the ship.

The boat rolled sideways, and Gregorie prayed one last prayer to Maman, letting her know how sorry he was that he could not retrieve the plants she needed. Then he told her he would surely see her in the afterlife.

Thirteen

Gregorie followed Gentille through the dunes, running to keep up. The rain continued to come down in sheets, perhaps a sign that their plan to reach France would fail at every turn, that Gregorie, who knew now that he had indeed been bitten by a vampire and must have ingested some of his blood, would never make it home to Maman, and Gentille would end up in jail for stealing her family's boat.

It had taken a long time to find the tiny outlet where Gentille wanted to hide *Second Wind*. With only a mere sapling of a tree to tie it to, Gregorie hoped (but doubted) it would remain secure. It would be a miracle if the sapling survived the wind and gushing rain of the storm.

And now that he and Gentille had reached the woods, they had to fight their way through trees swaying at drastic angles and branches attacking them like horse whips. Finally, as swollen as two human sponges, they arrived at the yellow bus, both of them dripping from their hair to their shoes.

Gentille pushed the strange, folded door in such a way

that it allowed them entrance. Cold, wet, and overwhelmed, Gregorie climbed the short, black steps.

Liam and Paul stretched across two of the dark-green seats in the very back. Paul's long calves hung over the end as he tossed a bright orange ball and caught it. Liam wore glasses and read a book; he seemed in no hurry for the storm to pass.

Paul let out a "Hey, yo!" Then said, "What the hell have you two tunnel rats been up to? Liam here's been worried sick."

"No I haven't. I mean, I was a little, I guess," he said, a flush of embarrassment coloring his face.

Gentille's wet sneakers squeaked down the aisle. She was careful not to step on any of the clothing and shoes strewn about the floor. "I'm sorry we worried you," she said, with a tremble in her voice. "So cold."

Gregorie followed after her, taking the seat beside the one she sat in.

"Grab that sweatshirt," Liam told him.

Even though he wasn't cold, he found the garment Liam referred to and put it on. It had a hood that he pulled up and tugged around his face. He would rather not speak to anyone now that he'd remembered what had happened to him and why he desired the blood.

Liam reached over and passed Gentille a blanket. "You two look horrible. What happened?"

Gregorie drew his knees into his chest and wished for his shell to climb into.

Gentille draped the blanket across her shoulders. "We're leaving," she said, biting her bottom lip as she eyed Liam.

"What, the bus, you mean?" Paul said, loudly. "You're moving out?"

"The island," she answered.

"Today? In this weather?" He scowled. "Whose idea was that?"

"I stole my family's boat," she said. "We're just crossing to the mainland."

"Benicia, no," said Liam rubbing his forehead as if what she said gave him a headache. "You can't. I won't let you. I can't believe *he* let you." He gestured to Gregorie and passed him a frown as well.

"He has to get back to his mother in France," she said. "She's sick . . . And I'm going to make a fresh start there. In a beautiful place far away from here."

Liam sought the view out the window and shook his head.

Paul grumbled. "You don't really think you're going to motor-boat all the way to France, do you?"

Gentille deflated. "No, Paul. We just need the boat to get off the island. I'm not a complete moron."

He tossed the orange ball in the air. "You have no money for the ferry, but you have enough for a flight to France?"

She turned away from Paul and spoke directly to Liam. Her voice became small when she said, "I have a debit card in a locker in Point Jeremiah."

Paul threw the orange ball against the bus's ceiling. It made a sharp smacking sound that rattled Gregorie's bones. "All the times we went hungry," Paul said, "and you had plenty of money right there, in Point Jeremiah. Okay, yeah, that makes a lot of sense."

"If I used the card while I was on the island, my parents would know exactly where I was and they'd come for me," Gentille replied. "But if I buy our plane tickets and fly out the same day, by the time they find out I've used the card, we'll be long gone."

"Good for you." Paul pitched the ball at the ceiling again. "Good luck. Thanks for stopping by."

"Stop throwing that stupid lacrosse ball," Liam said, raising his voice. "Benicia, tell me what's going on. Is this about Eli, did you run into him?"

"No. I told you before, it's not just about my brother. It's never been just about him. I have to get away . . . I have to save, uh—" She stopped, blinking back what appeared to be a sob forcing its way out of her throat.

The men eyed her closely in wait of whatever words she'd utter next.

"Yourself?" Paul said. "Your cat? *Who* do you have to save?"

She covered her mouth with her hand and took a shaky inhale. "Yes," she said, "myself."

Liam turned to the window. "There's no way I'm letting you leave in the middle of this storm," he said, "so you can forget that."

"I know we can't leave during the storm. I wouldn't have taken the boat today if I'd thought the storm was actually heading our way. Usually they blow out to sea."

Liam reached over the seat back between them and took her hand. "I could help you return the boat, you know. You can still change your mind."

"You know what I want to know," Paul said, tossing the ball in the air again, though not high enough to reach the ceiling. "What kind of hold does Greg here have on you?"

Gentille tilted her head and squinted as if casting an angry spell in Paul's direction. "What do you mean?"

"Ever since you met him, he's had some mesmerizing effect on you. You probably haven't noticed because that's how manipulation works—it's undetectable to the one under its spell."

Gregorie wanted to defend himself, but held back, waiting to see how Gentille would respond.

"Don't be an ass," she said.

Paul sat back and shrugged. "Okay, I won't. But you've never stolen your family's boat before. And until today, I haven't heard you mention a need to quote-unquote 'save, uh, yourself,' so, it sort of sounds like you're lying about that. But I'm sure I'm wrong."

"Maybe this was always my plan," she said, her escalating emotions making angles of her usually soft features. "Maybe I never told you because you have such a big fucking mouth full of annoying opinions!"

Paul nodded with a grimace, as if she'd stuck a needle in his ear. "That's fair. I can see that." He stroked his beard before flinging the ball at the ceiling again, making everyone jump.

Gregorie did not like this conversation. The friends should not be fighting about him and Gentille, and what they wanted to do. He stood and cleared his throat. "I'm going to leave now," he said. "I will be in my cave, Gentille, if you need me."

"What? No, you don't have to leave." She reached out and grabbed his arm. "Please, stay."

"The three of you should talk. I don't want to be the problem that makes you fight."

"He's right, Benicia," Liam said. "We *should* talk."

She turned to face Liam again, not saying or doing anything. Just looking at him.

Finally, she said, "Okay," in a gentle voice. "I'll stay here tonight, but I'll be at the cave at dawn. I still want to do this. I still want to go to France."

"*Moi aussi*," Gregorie said. "I am sorry for the trouble." He didn't want to be responsible for taking her away from her friends if she decided that's not what she wanted to do.

"Promise me you won't disappear," she called after him.

"*Jamais*," he said. Never.

Fourteen

Gregorie pressed his body in between the thin limbs and wiry vines of the cave's entrance and squeezed through its narrow corridor. His thoughts remained on the trip to France and whether Gentille would still want to go. He hoped so.

At the end of the short tunnel, he detected a glowing light and paused in the safety of the darkness. The cave walls came alive with the flickering flame of fire. He continued forward and spied a torch glowing on the far side, monstrous shadows spreading across the walls.

"*Oh la la*, I guess it's my lucky day."

The formidable, deep voice brought every one of Gregorie's nerves to attention. He whipped his head to the right and recoiled when he met a familiar piercing stare. Standing only yards away was the giant who had killed the ship's crew and then bitten him too. He didn't wear the waist-coat and stockings Gregorie remembered from that fateful night, just plain black pants and a soft, loose top, also black.

His horrible face, with its large, round eyes, long pointed nose, and rough jaundiced skin was unmistakable.

Have I suddenly gone mad?

"Fate has brought us back together," the giant said in a pleased, almost gentlemanly manner. "I knew I needed only be patient."

Gregorie's body seemed to have stalled. He stood several paces away, cowering like a mouse waiting for the hawk to swoop down and take him in its clutches.

"You are surprised to see me," the giant said with a subtle grin. "I understand. But it's not as surprising as one might presume. Think back to the very first time you arrived at this cave. You felt compelled to seek it out, did you not?"

Gregorie considered this. Liam had brought him to the cliffs. Had he felt compelled to be there? He remembered wanting to dig a hole . . . but when he neared the cliffs, his curiosity got the better of him. Gentille and Liam tried to stop him, but, yes, he *had* felt compelled to enter.

"If you think back to that day, I'm sure you'll agree that you were drawn to this place. Because that's how it works. The 'made' naturally seeks the 'maker.'"

"I *wasn't* seeking you," Gregorie said. "I'd hoped I would never see you again."

The corners of the vampire's mouth quirked.

Gregorie wrapped his arms around himself in an effort to stop the involuntary quaking of his body. "A friend brought me here. It had nothing to do with you."

He couldn't explain why he'd ventured into a dark place that might have led to a snake pit. And, worse, he could not deny that arriving at the cave had felt meant to be, as did the trunk he found inside. *His shell.*

The man moved closer. "Do you know who I am?" he asked, his horrible face becoming ever more angular thanks to shadows cast by the torch's flame. His full head of dark hair struck Gregorie as not quite right paired with such a hollow countenance.

He swallowed before answering. “The monster from the ship.”

The man laughed with hair-raising delight, the whites of his eyes outlined in a gruesome shade of blood red. “Yes, that is correct. I am the so-called ‘monster’ from the ship.” He paced the floor, and Gregorie sensed a slight falter in his step, just a hitch, barely decipherable. “My name is Reynaud. And you are Gregoire Babin. And you have no idea how pleased I am to find you.”

Gregorie stifled the urge to leap into his shell and slam the lid tight. But doing so would not save him, he knew.

“Because you want to kill me?” he asked.

“Kill you? Oh, *non, non, non, mon petit*. On the contrary, I very much want you to live.”

In spite of Reynaud’s apparent admiration, Gregorie did not believe him.

The giant circled the perimeter of the cave, and Gregorie, who stood at its center, turned in equal measure to keep him in direct sight.

“You have made your way to Wodge Island and come upon my hideaway. No doubt you’ve made use of my trunk,” Reynaud said, stroking his chin. “You have to admit that is a strange set of coincidences.”

He gestured to Gregorie’s shell. “You know what this is, don’t you? You know that your friend built it for me.”

“My f-friend?” he stammered.

“The woodworker in Saint-Suliac. I do hope that your trunk held up as well as this one has. I assume it did because if it had not, surely you would have become food for the sharks.”

Guillaume had made the trunk.

He’d been so excited about it, so proud of his work. The special mahogany, its smooth denseness, glassy to the touch. *Two trunks,* Gregorie remembered. *Guillaume had made two.*

"And you are here, on this island for what reason?" Gregorie asked.

"We summer here every year. Ever since we washed ashore in the 1700s after that fateful crossing of the Atlantic."

Had Reynaud said *we*? Perhaps Gregorie had misheard.

"You knew I would be here?" he asked.

Reynaud shook his head in a delighted manner. "I didn't know I'd ever see you again, but I had hoped. I had faith, as they say. And I can tell you that I am thrilled to have you here as my guest."

"Thrilled for what reason?" Gregorie asked. "You can bite anyone you like, so I don't understand why you care what I do."

"Oh yes, well, that is a good question. Let me explain." As he continued to walk a circle around Gregoire, Reynaud brought his pointer finger to his upper lip. "I have been a creature of the night for many years, many lifetimes, as a matter of fact. More than five centuries. And during this time I've committed a number of, let's call them 'not exactly *ethical* acts,' morally ambiguous in nature. I'm sure you know what I mean . . . " He paused to gaze knowingly in Gregorie's direction. "I noticed you've cut your milk teeth."

"My *milk teeth*?" Gregorie said, baffled.

Reynaud stepped toward him. "And is that a beating heart I hear?"

"All I know is that you have killed many people," Gregorie said, shuffling backward. "On *Le Chanceux* alone there were one hundred passengers and an entire crew."

The monster's steel-gray gaze flicked in his direction and held him with some invisible, mesmerizing power that paralyzed his limbs.

"I like to think of myself akin to the jaguar in the forest." Reynaud's cool, smooth voice hinted at the cruelty lurking below. "The jaguar must take certain actions in order to survive. It is only natural that he seeks prey. If he wants to live, if he desires to continue his reign as king of the forest, he must eat. I am the jaguar. I must eat. How I catch my prey, however, is up to me. And sometimes I . . . " He paused here. "Well, let's just say, I become bored with the same old *methods*. Sometimes I indulge my creative side."

Gregorie shuddered at whatever that might mean.

"Suffice it to say," Reynaud said slowly, "the accumulation of my actions has me worried for my soul."

"Your soul has nothing to do with me," Gregorie said.

"Oh, but it does. You and I both know that it does. Because I saw you. On the ship. I saw what you can do. I know what you are." His face portrayed a horrible mix of life and death, human and inhuman. "*Un ange de la mort*," he said. An angel of death.

Gregorie remembered the dying crewman on the deck of the ship. He remembered the hiss that whispered through his ears just after he'd released the man's soul and said, "Go with grace." Reynaud had been there, watching in the shadows. *That's why he let me live! Reynaud is worried for his own damned soul.*

"If it should come time for me to perish," Reynaud said calmly, "my soul cannot descend. It may be tattered and rotten or a mere wisp of dust at this point, but I am a being who enjoys the finer things in life. There is only one place I want my soul to go. It cannot go to hell and live in the dungeons of Satan or the infernos of Hades. If the time comes—or perhaps I should say, *when* the time comes, because most of my kind come to an eventual end—you, my friend, must reach in and save my poor, tattered soul. I know you can do it. And that is why you are here. That is why, when the ship went down, I made sure you would survive."

"*You* made sure I would survive?" Gregorie didn't understand. His shell had been the thing that protected him.

A sudden rustling of leaves at the cave's entrance drew his attention. Someone was coming in. A young woman in a white dress that reached to the floor entered carrying a bouquet of blue and white wildflowers. The rain and wind had made wiry, vivacious spirals of her hair. Her damp skin gleamed a pleasing shade of brown, though with unusual, murky undertones, and she padded upon bare feet.

It couldn't be.

Gregorie's nerves prickled as the young woman's attention shifted from the flowers to him. Her gaze slammed into him, threatened to topple him, as the light of the torch brought a devious sparkle to her odd shade of red-brown eyes. With this connection, this unexpected meeting, Gregorie's bones seemed to crumble like dry earth under his skin.

Michaelangela?

This was the girl he'd longed for, prayed to the moon to bring back, cried for, and searched for. For nine years she'd been gone, and he'd feared the worst. Yet here she was, just as young, beautiful, and graceful as he remembered. Still a teenaged girl in a white cotton dress. Still opting not to wear shoes. Still the one Gregorie had loved since childhood. And yet she was horribly, frightfully different.

What had Reynaud done to her?

Gregorie stared at her for what seemed like a long time before his hand levitated in her direction, desiring to touch her, to test if she were real. "Is it you?" he asked.

When she didn't answer right away, he turned back to Reynaud. "What have you done to her? Is she not allowed to speak?"

"On the contrary," Reynaud said dully, as if bored by the situation. "She speaks very well. In several languages, as a matter of fact. Perhaps she is not as happy to see you as you are to see her."

The young woman in front of him was not the person Gregorie knew and loved. Not the one he'd wanted to marry. Her cheeks were full and her complexion golden brown, her body, lean and strong and tall in that way she'd always appeared taller than she actually was, but this person observed the world with a gloom-ridden attitude and a suspicious, resourceful, perhaps even malevolent, perspective. Everything Gregorie sensed about her told him she was not the Michaelangela he once knew and loved.

The girl he knew laughed easily, her presence rife with natural warmth. She loved to joke with him, sing silly songs, play games they made up. This was Michaelangela if her feisty spirit had been flattened under a leaden blanket of sadness. Or, perhaps, something worse. Perhaps something evil.

"I don't know you," she said in a tepid, aloof tone surely meant to hurt him.

Gregorie continued to stare, the whole of his body alive with the kind of excitement that courses through one's veins after something awful, like an accident, has occurred.

"I am Gregorie, and you are Michaelangela," he said. "Your father, Guillaume, was clinging to his last shred of hope for your return when I last saw him. I told him that one day I'd find you and bring you back. I'm going home, to Saint-Suliac, back to Maman. You must come with me."

At this, Reynaud broke into laughter. Gregorie gave him a questioning look, then turned back to Michaelangela, who blinked at him with disdain. Was she suspicious of what he'd said—or maybe she simply found him ridiculous.

"Don't worry, your mother will not be angry," he told her. "She will be relieved to have you home. She was devastated after you left. And your father, he never stopped thinking about you—"

"Stop!" Michaelangela's back hunched like the hackles of an animal preparing for attack.

Gregorie cowered back and then froze in place.

Perhaps she really had left home because she'd wanted to.

"I'm sorry if this angers you," he told her in a gentle voice, "but you promised we'd leave together. You promised, and then you left without warning. *We were going to be married*," he said, forcing the words through quivering lips.

Her eyes flicked to Reynaud, then back to the bouquet in her hands. "That was a promise that became impossible to keep."

So now he knew: Reynaud had taken her. Reynaud had stolen Michaelangela from her home!

"We're going back to France, *mes amis et moi*. You must come with us," he said, desperate for her to show some sign of agreement. "We will go home to Maman and Guillaume, to Saint-Suliac, where we can—"

"Please stop," Reynaud interrupted. "You poor, ridiculous child, I can't bear to listen to any more of this."

Gregorie turned to find Reynaud wearing a fang-revealing scowl. "Your Maman is nothing but dust under a gravestone by now."

"You have been to Saint-Suliac?" Gregorie asked. "You know this to be true?"

"I don't have to go there to know it's true," Reynaud said. "I am certain she's dead. As are all the humans who lived in the eighteenth century."

"I don't understand."

"You left your home in Saint-Suliac over three hundred years ago," Michaelangela told him. "You've been away for three hun—"

"This cannot be!" Gregorie shouted.

"What Reynaud says is true," Michaelangela muttered.

"That's impossible. How are you still alive?" His voice flared with accusation.

She fixed her glassy, red-brown eyes on him. She was incredibly still, revealing no emotion whatsoever. "Same way you are."

It doesn't make sense. None of it makes sense.

"I turned Michaelangela," Reynaud said. "Just as I turned you."

"*Non. Non!*" Gregorie shouted. "You haven't turned me. I never drank vampire blood, and I am not turned. I am Gregorie, same as I have always been."

"Of course you are," Reynaud said. "Only you *are* a vam—"

"I don't believe you!" Gregorie's panic spiraled from the soles of his feet to the top of his skull. He was not a monster! He was an angel of death. He didn't drink human blood. More important, he had *never* soiled his soul by doing bad deeds, and he never would. One day his soul would light the moon, just like Maman said it would.

Unable to stand their presence any longer, he entered the tunnel and ran back into the wet, blustering soup of the storm. He tore across the beach, aiming straight for the charcoal-gray horizon, not stopping until he'd splashed into the ocean's edge. "Maman!" he shouted so forcefully his stomach wrung like a wet sponge. "Maman!" His voice mixed with wicked gusts of wind that pulled at his hair and pitched the rain like pellets at his face.

He dropped to his knees and implored the ocean to help him get back home. Thick, writhing clouds blanketed the sky and covered any evidence of the moon, any comfort he might derive from the sight of his grandfather.

"*Je suis désolé, Maman. Je suis désolé,*" he said. I'm sorry, Maman. I'm sorry.

Afterward, when he had used up all of the energy raging at the world around him, he fell back on the sand and took in the infinite sky above.

It wasn't until then that he wondered, *Where have I been for so long?*

Fifteen

The Year 1724: Atlantic Ocean

Knocked off his feet and face down to the swamped deck of *Le Chanceux*, Gregorie prayed to Maman. The monster had left him without warning, and for this Gregorie thanked the heavens. He would rather be washed overboard and sink to the bottom of the sea than suffer whatever fate the giant had planned for him.

But then, the brute reappeared, that same limp in his step as he carried two sizable trunks, one under each of his arms. The one on the right side wore a thick metal chain secured with a brass lock the size of a human heart. Was it some kind of treasure? Or had he simply packed his things?

Reynaud set the two chests on the deck in front of Gregorie, then opened the one that was not bound and pulled out a second lock and chain.

Gregorie leapt to his feet and thrust himself backward, into the wall of the ship.

"Get in," the man said, gesturing to the open trunk. "You're a small fellow. It will suit you. This is the best wood money can buy. It's waterproof, nothing to worry about. If it were hot temperatures in a dry climate, you'd become dried fruit, but cold temperatures in a wet climate won't hurt you." He said it with a smile, as if they were two people having an everyday conversation on a ship that was not about to capsize.

Gregorie was sure the giant was mad.

"Get in," he said more forcefully this time, his kindness disappearing under an angry scowl.

There was no way Gregorie was getting into that box.

"You'll die if you don't," Reynaud said. "You'll be thrown into the sea, and you're not strong enough to fend off whatever you encounter. The fish will eat you. And if they don't, the waves will eventually dash your bones into the rocks and the reef. Get in, and I promise you'll eventually wash up on the shore. The box won't float, but it won't plant itself either. The current will push you along, bit by bit, and one day you'll make it to land. You'll be safe."

Gregorie planned to fling himself overboard, but when he made the move, the wind pressed against him so forcibly he had no choice but to stay put.

Reynaud grabbed him by the back of his shirt and tugged with such strength that Gregorie's neck suffered a severe jerking motion. His skinny arms and legs flailed before meeting with the monster's ungiving flesh, much like hitting a stone wall. The creature handled him as if he weighed no more than a doll, pressing his limbs together and rolling him up the way he might a tablecloth folded into a basket.

Gregorie shouted, "Wait! *Non!* Stop!" as the top of the trunk came crashing over his head. The sound of the heavy chain knocked the walls that surrounded him as he imagined the giant winding it around and fastening the lock. He shouted, "Why are you doing this to me?" and attempted to pound his fists into the wood, though there was no room for that kind of motion.

A moment later he experienced a quick drop followed by bobbing movements. Muted gurgles and gushes replaced the howls of raging wind and seething squeals of a ship on the brink of collapse. He imagined the trunk floating for a few minutes before making its descent toward the bottom of the sea.

After that, his own breath mingled with a new kind of silence that settled in around him: a slow, watery persistent lull. He was alive. In a locked box. In the sea. And that triggered a swelling panic that rose like a storm inside of him, a storm with no place to go, and for a short time, he became a hurricane trapped in a box.

"I am in the sea!" he cried. "Help me, Maman! Please, help me!"

Gentle swipes, bumps, rattles, and scrapes came and went.

And Gregorie waited. He waited for the monster to collect him.

He waited for the trunk that protected him to be dashed upon the rocks.

He waited for the slow-lulling motion to end.

For years, this went on, day by day by day, until his hope for this existence to end dried up, and a boundless stretch of darkness and time spread over him like a shroud.

Once in a while he wondered, *How am I still alive? Is this purgatory? Perhaps I am in hell.*

But even these thoughts in due course thinned and flattened, and eventually passed away, until Gregorie had nothing left but time. Nothing but nothingness. Nothing but darkness.

And so he became the mollusk inside of the shell.

Sixteen

Gregorie would not return to the cave where Reynaud and Michaelangela remained. Instead, he stayed at the foot of the ocean, fearing that if he tried to go anywhere, they would hunt him down.

He didn't want to be alone. He would have much rather been in the company of Gentille, and maybe Liam, and perhaps even Paul. But he couldn't go to the yellow bus. He could not lead Reynaud to his friends.

The rain had stopped, and he continued to stare out to sea. He wished for the wind to carry him over the vast ocean to the place where cobblestone paths led to houses with brightly painted doors and bunches of flowers in window boxes. No matter what had happened, he would always be Maman's son, and Saint-Suliac would be his home.

Hours passed before Michaelangela approached him. The sight of her brought warring feelings of eagerness and dread, peace and anxiety, comfort and pain. If only she could be the same girl he once knew, then he could bring her back home with him and at least they would have each other. At least they would have a life of some sort together. But *non*.

"We're going out," she said in the lackluster way she had of speaking. Instead of meeting his eye, she stared out to sea. Was it longing he detected in her expression? Sadness? Regret? Or maybe just boredom.

"Do you want to come with us?" Her tone made it clear that she didn't care either way.

He supposed Reynaud had ordered her to invite him.

He didn't give her an answer. Instead, he studied her once-joyful face in search of a hint of the person he knew and loved.

"Saying nothing is a choice," she said, bowing her head as she pushed some sand around with her bare toes, "so I will assume your answer is no."

"What happened to you?" he asked.

She stilled herself. "Reynaud told you. He took me away. He turned me," she said, her words clipped with impatience.

"But how can you stay with him? Why haven't you escaped by now?"

This time she used a hostile tone to answer: "Just be glad you were the lucky one who became lost at sea."

He couldn't imagine how that made him lucky.

"I was in a trunk too," she said, "but he made sure to hold on to mine."

The second trunk. The locked one. Michaelangela had been on *Le Chanceux*.

"So, I'm right," he said gently. "You couldn't get away. You would have come home if it were possible. Reynaud was, is, too strong."

She shook her head. Gregorie assumed words eluded her, but then she said, "*Non*. Or, I don't know. Maybe."

"Maybe he's too strong? Or maybe you would have come back?"

Her eyes hardened and brows grew sharp. "I tried to tell you. All those years ago. You didn't listen to me, Gregorie. Just like my mother didn't listen to me, and my father didn't want to hear me. I *wanted* to go away."

"So did I!" he said, doing his best to keep his frustration in check. "We were going to move together."

"If I had stayed with you, we would have been married, and we would have left Saint-Suliac, but we wouldn't have gone far. You wanted to stay close to your Maman. I longed to get away from mine. You knew that. What you didn't want to believe was that I also wanted to see the world—that being able to do so was just as important as marrying you."

He'd never thought too much of her desire to travel. He'd figured they would visit different places every summer. But certainly travel wasn't as important as being married was.

"You wanted *me*," he said, surprised by how bold this statement sounded.

He reached out and clasped her hand, noting how she did not return the favor.

She raised her chin, though her aura seemed fatigued, or perhaps disinterested. "When I was a girl, I loved the boy next door. But when I grew up, I wanted to leave Saint-Suliac, and I dreamed of going to London, Hong Kong, Australia, the Caribbean.

"Foolishly, I loved the idea of adventure," she continued, "but I am no longer a little girl or a young woman or even an old woman who has not seen the world. I am a creature of the night, and I no longer love anything. Maybe the girl I was let you down, but those days are long gone. They don't matter anymore."

At that, his hand opened, and hers slipped out of his grasp.

"They matter to me," he said, glaring at her.

"You don't know me," she said.

The words chilled him even more than his damp clothing did.

"You want to know why I stay with Reynaud?" she said. "Because, as I said, doing nothing is a choice. I did nothing about my undead life for so long that it has become the only way for me now. I need blood to survive, and believe me when I say I *never* go without. Nor do I want to."

At that, he stumbled internally, shocked by her statement.

"So, I'll ask you again," she said, "do you want to come out with us tonight? You'll need to think hard before giving me an answer, for this night will be the one that determines what you will become for the rest of your afterlife."

Gregorie hated to imagine Michaelangela seizing an innocent person and wrenching their neck back the way Reynaud had wrenched his. Her face, though haunting and beautiful, appeared gaunt with deep eye sockets and hollowed cheeks, vaguely skeletal from certain angles. *Is that what the hunger for blood looks like?* he wondered. To any human in a dimly lit room, she could pass for one of the ordinary people in this world, perhaps suffering from lack of sun and fresh air the same way he did when he'd first arrived.

"You're going out tonight to kill someone?"

Her pained expression implored him to understand. "I *always* need blood. And so will you if you're not careful."

"I will never drink it," he said.

"Of course you won't," she said with surrender. "You were always so good. Such a good person. Helping others. Healing them. I had hoped I'd never see you again. I'd hoped you'd never come to know what I've become."

A fire flared in his mind. All this time, he'd wished to see her, but she did not feel the same way. "If you don't like what you're doing, you should stop doing it," he said.

Her smile was the saddest he'd ever seen. "Once you drink blood, there's no turning back. You never stop wanting it."

"But that's not true. You can drink fish blood," he said. "Or deer."

"Is that what you do?"

He felt ashamed, like an adolescent who'd just revealed his childish ways.

"Reynaud and I will be back before dawn." She engaged him in a prolonged stare and then raised her brows before turning away.

Gregorie wondered if it was an attempt to impart an unspoken message.

"And?" he said.

"And what?"

"I should go, run, hide?"

"Goodbye, Gregorie."

Questions raced through his mind, as he watched her follow the curved edge of the cove, moving away at great speed. He supposed she was trying to tell him he should get away while he still could, to save himself before they returned.

He wanted to believe that she was.

Gregorie sensed Reynaud's presence, and when he turned around, a tall, dark figure walked toward him, reaching him in no time, much faster than a human would have.

"I am not going with you," Gregorie said.

Reynaud eyed him skeptically. "That's fine. Stay home if you're not hungry. Have some alone time, as they call it, but don't forget, you belong to me. Fate wills it so. And you love Michaelangela. In time, the three of us can go back to France, if you like. We can go anywhere you want, but we *will* stay together. Tonight, you may have lost Maman, but you have gained a new family."

A family? *Non*. Not at all. If anything his new family was Gentille, and he could think of nothing else but telling her and the guys to get to the mainland before Reynaud drained every human on the island.

"France is where I want to go. And I would like to leave now," Gregorie said.

"But we've only just arrived, *mon fils*," Reynaud said with a chuckle. "Let us spend a couple of days or weeks seaside. It's my intention to kick back and enjoy myself, as they say. There's no hurry now that you know no one waits for you in Saint-Suliac."

The hurtful words flashed like a blade through Gregorie's chest. He wished it were a real blade so he could grab it and turn it on Reynaud. He envisioned stabbing the vampire's black, rotting heart.

Reynaud easily caught up to Michaelangela, and they continued toward town together. He, in his dark pants and top; her, in her white dress to her ankles. The two of them appeared tall and proud, moving with otherworldly elegance and an aura of power. Would they lure some innocent human to their death? Would they at least be kind about it, making it quick and painless, or would Reynaud torture his victim, as he "indulged his creative side"?

Gregorie watched them, his hatred of Reynaud circling his mind, growing with every turn, as he tried not to hate Michaelangela as well. The pressure inside him grew, and his vision blurred. For a moment, he viewed the world through a strange red veil, and a sudden rush of heat filled his chest, his heart beating double time. He didn't know what was happening. He thought he might break down and cry, but then all at once the teeth set within his upper jaw shifted again. The gums tingled and then burned painfully as the awful need for blood reared up and tugged at his throat. Gregorie prepared to be pulled in some particular direction, driven by an animalish scent that would inspire the hunt, but when he breathed in deeply, he smelled nothing but sea spray.

The desire for blood eased back, though his fangs remained.

What did it mean? Was his body preparing him to become a full-fledged vampire? He wouldn't do it. He would defy his body. *It will be mind over matter*, he told himself. He didn't care what kind of teeth he grew. Nothing had changed, and nothing would. He would make sure of that.

Then he remembered the "terrible need" and how the scent of animal blood had gripped him so relentlessly. It was hard to believe he'd be able to retain control should his body betray him by wanting human blood.

But he couldn't sit around contemplating what-ifs. Not with Reynaud and his plan to remain on Wodge Island for a time.

Gentille and the guys must leave. That much was clear. But Gregorie couldn't go to them now. Couldn't risk being followed or leaving behind a trail Reynaud could later scent. So much had happened and was still happening: Maman was dead, Michaelangela had been taken, his own body was changing, and his friends were in danger. A feeling of absolute helplessness overwhelmed him. He longed for safety, for comfort, for his past life in Saint-Suliac. As he walked back to the cave, he decided he would climb into his shell for just a little while, just until he figured out what to do next.

Seventeen

"Gregorie, Gregorie! Are you here?"

He jolted out of his mental stupor and sprang upward, banging his head and neck against the top of his shell as he stood. Gentille had said she'd come at dawn. They planned to leave the island. How could he have forgotten? Michaelangela and Reynaud would be back at dawn as well.

"Don't come in here," he shouted.

He ran toward the entrance intending to meet her halfway through the tunnel, but Gentille was already there, in her slap-slap sandals, short shirt, and long, billowy skirt.

She put a hand over her eyes and spun around. "Why? Are you not dressed?"

"*Oui*, you have caught me . . . in my drawers," he said.

"Sorry. Get dressed. I have to tell you something."

Her voice lacked the usual optimism, so he figured it was bad news. Perhaps she didn't want to leave the island with him. Paul and Liam had talked her out of going to France.

He backed up a few steps and waited maybe two seconds before he said, "Okay, I am here. Let's talk outside."

She turned. "No, wait. I have to tell you something important."

"*Oui*, what is it?" he said, tempering his urge to insist she leave immediately.

She studied his face and said, "Is everything okay?"

"Yes, just, what do you need to tell me?"

"We really have to get you a phone for emergencies," she said.

He wouldn't know what to do with a phone, but he said yes anyway, growing more desperate to get her out of there.

"There was a double murder," she said. "Last night on East Beach. The police chief's wife and his son are dead. They were last seen at Tyler's Tavern for game night."

The hair on the back of his neck stood up.

Liam shouted from outside. "Is he there? Did you find him?"

"Yes, he's here," Gentille called back. "Come in, Liam. There are no snakes."

"No, don't come in," Gregorie shouted. "You must leave," he told Gentille. "Both of you. And Paul too. You must get off the island as fast as you can."

She smiled a little, and when he didn't return the favor, her face flattened with worry. "You aren't kidding?"

He shook his head and sought out his feet.

"And what about you? Won't you be coming with us?"

"*Non. Non*, I can't. I've changed my mind. I can't leave right now."

Her mouth dropped open. "You have to be joking."

"*Non*. I'm sorry," he said, grabbing his shock of overgrown bangs and raking them back. "You need to get to your boat. Take Liam and Paul with you. You should be with them." The words kept rolling out, thoughts he'd had last night and had planned to recite in a sober manner recklessly flew past his lips. But there was no time to deliver them soberly. If she didn't leave, Reynaud would bite her and turn her, or kill her, and he couldn't let that happen. If she left now, Liam and Paul would be able to keep her safe. They understood this strange world and how to survive in it far better than Gregorie did. Gregorie didn't belong here. He didn't belong with them.

"Is this about what Paul said yesterday?" Gentille asked, her mouth in a scowl. "Because I talked to him, and now he understands. Both he and Liam have given me their blessing on our plans for France, not that I need it. I can make my own decisions, obviously."

"I don't remember what Paul said," he muttered. "All I know is that you must—"

"Wait a minute," Gentille whispered, her lips quivering. "You didn't . . . oh my god, Gregorie, you couldn't have. Last night, where were you?" She froze, a realization bubbling to the top of her head. "Did you have something to do with those murders?" She covered her mouth with her hand as if sorry she'd spoken out loud.

Liam showed up just in time to hear her. "Why would he?" he said, planting his hands on his hips as he stepped up close to Gentille, his arm muscles bulging.

Gregorie didn't know how to answer that question, as stunned as he was.

"He wouldn't," Gentille said, nudging Liam back a step. "I—I don't know why I said that."

"You two have been hiding something," Liam said. "Tell me what it is."

"You must go now." Gregorie's panic grew with every second they remained in the cave. Michaelangela said they'd return at dawn, and faint morning light was seeping through the openings at the top of the cave walls. "How light is it outside?"

"What?" Liam said. "The sun's just starting to rise."

"Okay, okay," Gregorie said. "I want to be alone. Please go. Please get off the island. Go wherever you like. Just go."

Gentille's face fell into complete confusion.

"Please, Gentille," he begged her, his heart pounding in desperation. "It isn't safe here."

"You know something about those murders," she said.

"What I know is that we cannot go to France together." He paused, wishing he could take back what he'd just said. But he couldn't. Reynaud would return at dawn. "I cannot be your friend anymore. It isn't safe. You must leave now." He nudged her toward the exit.

"I'm not going until you tell me what happened," she said, pushing forward.

A stunned silence hung between them. The only sound was the huffing of Gentille's angry breath. Her expression was one of disappointment. Anger. Determination. Finally she looked away. Crinkling her nose, she said, "Whose flowers are those?"

The wildflowers Michaelangela had brought in the night before lay in the middle of the cave floor, wilted and discolored.

Gentille walked past Gregorie and gathered them up.

He followed behind her. "They're no one's. You must leave."

"Come on, Benicia," Liam said. "He's made it pretty clear what he wants. And we need to move the boat before someone discovers it."

"No, Liam," she said. "There are things you don't understand—"

"I'm sure there are, and you can tell me on the way." Suddenly he grabbed her around her waist and lifted her body over his shoulder, then turned and started walking.

"Good, good," Gregorie shouted. "Take her. Hurry!"

"Are you serious right now?" she screamed, kicking her

legs and pounding Liam's back with the wilted flower bouquet spraying little white petals like water droplets upon the cave floor.

Liam wobbled a bit as he carried her toward the exit, bumping the side wall before they passed out of sight. Gentille shouted, "Put me down, damn you. Ouch. . . . Oh my god, Liam!" The rustle of leaves told Gregorie they'd reached the vines and then there was a thump, and both of them began to curse.

Gregorie couldn't stand the sound of their angry voices. This was his fault. He ran to them. "Stop, stop, please. I have to tell you something. It's very bad."

They'd both fallen to the ground. Gentille's skirt was covered with debris, and Liam's cheek, smudged with dirt.

"I knew it," Gentille said, struggling to stand in the confined space. "You know something about the murders."

"I'm not sure. Maybe."

"What the hell," Liam said, his hair flopped out of its usual neat part. "Why would you?"

"I told you there are things you don't know," Gentille said.

Gregorie gave Liam a hand up. "I will tell you everything, but we have to leave now. We need to go someplace safe."

While Liam pressed through the narrow opening between cliff walls, Gentille grabbed Gregorie's hand. She squeezed so hard that it hurt, but he didn't care. He was just happy to be with his friends.

In the shadowy gray-pink light of dawn, the three of them climbed the dunes that led to the cemetery.

"Let's see if the church is open," Gentille said. "No one will be there at this hour, and vampires can't enter, right?"

Gregorie shrugged. "Is that what they say?"

"You know, holy water and all that . . . "

Gregorie didn't think anything of entering the church until he was already inside. Then he began to feel self-conscious and strange, as if someone above might consider him a dark element soiling a sacred place with his presence.

But that wasn't true. He was an angel of death, not a vampire.

They sat on a pew in the back, where Gregorie told them everything he remembered about his stormy voyage across the Atlantic. How the ship's crew and its passengers perished one by one, and how the giant of a man attacked him and tried to drop blood down his throat. How that same giant later shoved him into the trunk that he would eventually refer to as "his shell."

"I left France in the 1700s," he told them. "I was twenty-six years old."

At first Gentille simply stared. Then as if emerging from a hypnotic state, she laughed and said, "Well, I guess that explains your strange underwear."

Liam sat back, quiet. He failed to see the humor in it. "Are you guys messing with me right now? What are you saying exactly?"

"We are not messing with you," Gregorie said. "And Maman is dead," he told Gentille. "I'll never see her again."

"Oh, Gregorie, I'm so sorry." She reached across the pew and took him in a hug.

"So, wait," Liam interrupted, "you're saying that this guy, Reynaud, is a vampire? A real, live . . . You're saying that he actually drinks human blood?"

"*Oui*," Gregorie said. "He drank mine."

Liam's complexion paled. "And last night he killed the police chief's wife and son?"

"I don't know. Maybe. He is very old and very strong, and

he took Michaelangela from her home. Though, she says she wanted to go," he muttered.

"*Your* Michaelangela?" Gentille said. "The girl you grew up with? The one you love?"

The sadness of losing Michaelangela dropped over him like a bout of exhaustion. Suddenly his bones became too heavy to move, and the darkness inside of him threatened to snuff out the light. "She is here too. Reynaud turned her. They have traveled together ever since."

"And what about you?" Liam said. "If you're like Reynaud, you need blood too."

"*Non*, I never have."

"That doesn't make sense," he said. "How are you still alive?"

Gentille, put her hands out to stop Liam from saying more. "Gregorie is repulsed by the idea of drinking human blood. So far he's only had animal blood."

"The deer that first night," Liam said. "That's why your shirt was covered with it."

"Reynaud says fate brought me to him," Gregorie said. "That no matter what I do, fate will always bring me to him. That's why I ended up here, on this island. And that's why you have to get away from me. He won't kill me because I am an angel of death. One day he'll need me to save his soul. But he will kill you. Or steal you away."

Liam squinted. "Angel of death? What the hell does that mean?"

"He'll explain later," Gentille said, placing her hand on Liam's chest. Then she faced Gregorie. "Listen, it's going to be all right. We'll stay together. We have to. I'm not going to let you fight him alone. And, oh my god, I just thought of something," she said, with open-mouthed awe. "I don't know why I didn't think of it before. Paul can help us."

Gregorie frowned. "Paul?"

"Shit, yes!" Liam's words flew up to the rafters. "Paul will know exactly what to do about Reynaud."

"But we can't tell him about me," Gregorie said, turning to Gentille. "You promised you wouldn't tell him."

"He doesn't have to know," she said, taking his hand in hers once again. "It will be fine. Stop worrying and come on. There's no time to waste."

Gregorie followed her out of the church but not without reluctance. Gentille may have trusted Paul, but he never would.

~

INSIDE THE YELLOW BUS, their tall, bearded friend lounged at the far end, where they'd found him the afternoon before. With his back against the wall, his long legs stretched across the seat, calves and feet hanging over by a foot or more. Gentille had entered first and led Gregorie up the aisle. They sat together in the seat beside Paul's, with Liam taking one behind them.

While Paul listened carefully to Gregorie describe Reynaud and how he'd arrived at Wodge Island the night before, he tossed his orange lacrosse ball in the air and caught it. "So, what you're telling me is that we're dealing with a member of the undead from the eighteenth century?"

Gregorie nodded. "I believe he's even older. But I don't know for sure."

Paul stroked his beard. "Okay, let me think this through. A vampire of that caliber is far too strong for the average human to fight. The best thing would be to avoid confrontation altogether. You can't beat this guy." He wore a serious stare that dared Gregorie to argue. "The plan should be to get to the boat as soon as possible and tear out of here as fast as we can."

"Yes," Gregorie said with enthusiasm. "Good idea. The three of you must leave right now."

"Whoa, whoa, that's not what I said. Won't you be joining us?"

"I can't. It is . . . not a good idea," Gregorie mumbled.

Paul breathed in and then let out a breath that wreaked of annoyance. "Pray tell, what secrets are you hiding, my friend?"

Gregorie turned to Gentille. What would he do now?

She whispered, "Just tell him. It will be all right."

"Yes, please spit it out," Paul said in his usual harsh tone.

"Reynaud wants me to join him and Michaelangela and . . . " Gregorie hesitated.

"Go on," Paul said.

"He says that I am destined to be with him, that fate wills it so."

"Well, that's interesting. Why would that be, I wonder?"

"I have no idea."

"Is it because you drank his blood?" Paul's hairy eyebrows reached for the top of his head and remained there as if stuck.

"*Non!* I never did."

But that was a lie. He remembered emerging from what he thought was going to be his death and finding Reynaud's bloody arm hovering over his face.

"Gregorie is telling the truth," Gentille said.

"And yet he's acquainted with a man and a woman who have both survived as vampires for hundreds of years. Seems too good to be true, doesn't it?"

"I'm just old." Gregorie's voice shook. "It was the shell. It was like hibernation. It kept me alive."

Paul forced a loud breath through his nose.

The others sat in silence.

"I am *not* a vampire," Gregorie said as sternly as he knew how.

His three friends averted their eyes and kept their thoughts to themselves.

"Have I ever tried to drink your blood?" he asked.

"He never has," Gentille said. "I've seen him gag at the thought of it."

"Well, that's lucky for us," Paul said, "but the situation could change. If he so much as samples the blood of a human, it will be all that he desires from that day forward."

"I would *never* kill a human. I am an angel of death. I must remain pure if my soul is to one day light the moon."

"An angel of death?" Paul said. "But that's basically a vampire, isn't it?" Before Gregorie could respond, he said, "Would you object to my looking into your mouth?"

Liam leaned in, curious, and then Gentille did as well. Gregorie didn't want them to see the change in his teeth—but what reason could he give not to open his mouth? With no other option, he did as Paul asked.

Paul took his phone from his back pocket and switched on the flashlight, then guided the beam into Gregorie's mouth. Gentille gasped while Liam said, "Holy!"

"Oh, well, now," said Paul, "those are quite sharp, aren't they? I guess that's how you got that cut on your bottom lip."

"What cut? What do you see?" Gregorie said, then snapped his mouth closed.

"Your canine teeth have settled in, I'm afraid."

"That doesn't mean anything," Gregorie said, remembering Reynaud's comment about his milk teeth and the odd sensation he'd experienced on the beach, when his fangs grew into place. They never stayed there for long, however. He'd always felt them retreat. Still, the situation had reached a serious level, he realized, and when he next spoke, it was in a steady voice steeped in urgency. "I will never kill another person. I swear on Maman's soul."

Paul froze, seemingly stunned by the weight of this declaration. "I guess we'll have to take your word for it. But don't be mistaken, my friend, you are a vampire. You have all the working parts."

Paul's words split whatever it was on the inside that had kept Gregorie's human part separate from his vampire part. He wanted to deny the facts. To argue that it didn't matter Reynaud had bitten him and fed him drops of blood, or even that fangs had grown in where his ordinary teeth used to be. He wanted to argue that he was still human. He considered all of the truths he might point to, to convince them that he was not what Paul said he was, but it was a losing argument.

A strange sense of calm fell over him. He eased back and made space for yet another thought: yes, he might be a vampire, but he was also *not* a killer. The two facts could simultaneously be true.

"I trust Gregorie," Gentille said. "You don't know him like I do."

Gregorie straightened his spine. "No matter what I am, I am *not* a monster. I am still Gregorie Babin. Angel of death from Saint-Suliac, France. This is what I am." He set his jaw and made fists of his hands.

Silence fell upon the three friends, who seemed to hold their breath.

Paul threw the ball and caught it. "Okay," he said. "I hear you."

Gregorie drooped with relief. "But do you believe me?"

"I believe that *you* believe you," he said. "And I don't know, maybe when you're nearby we'll just have to wear garlic around our necks. No worries," he said, back to his sarcastic tone.

"Well, I for one," Gentille said, "am more than willing to do that for Gregorie." She placed her hand on his shoulder. "We all have problems, Paul. We all have issues that we deal with on a daily basis. You know that as well as I do. As a matter of fact—" She stopped speaking abruptly and drew a sudden, tense breath. "There's something I need to tell all of you."

Gregorie didn't like how she appeared sheepish and pale.

"I didn't say anything before, Gregorie, and I should have. It's important, and you need to know. Just . . . " She paused there as she fidgeted where she sat. Finally, she cleared her throat. "There's something else I have to do before we leave for France."

Tears spilled over the hills of her cheeks, and Gregorie fought the urge to wipe them away.

Liam rested a hand on her shoulder. "What is it? You can tell us."

"It's my little sister. I can't leave her alone with them."

"Sister?" Paul said. "When did you get a sister?"

"She's only three. And she's why I've stayed on the island. I've been keeping an eye on her from a distance." Gentille raised her gaze to meet Liam, then Gregorie, her chin trembling. "I can't leave her. So if you don't want her to come with us to France, you have to tell me now. She and I will find another way."

"Of course I want her to come with us," Gregorie said. "Your sister must be with you."

Paul made an angry spitting sound. "A toddler's making the trip? That's gonna complicate things tenfold. You might wanna rethink it, considering a giant vampire will be tracking us."

"I can't do that, Paul," Gentille said through clenched teeth. Her body seemed to be on the verge of eruption, her middle trembling as she struggled to keep whatever boiled inside contained. A shade of volcanic red rose up her neck and settled into her flushed cheeks. "She's mine," she said, with a gasp. "Okay? Her name is Mia, and she's *my* daughter. I won't leave without her."

Paul and Liam sank back, their faces numb, jaws slack, as if the news disabled them. Why weren't they happy for her? She had a child—that was a wonderful thing. Their silence made them seem angry, but Gregorie didn't know why. His fangs began to protrude the same way they had when Reynaud had upset him. All he could think about was protecting Gentille and her daughter.

Why would she lie about having a child?

Liam whispered, "Was it your brother?"

Gentille sobbed, the sadness gushing out of her.

"He better hope he never runs into me because I will *kill* that little piece of shit," Paul muttered. He grabbed the orange ball, squeezing it until his knuckles turned white.

Gregorie didn't dare open his mouth to speak, lest he reveal a fang.

Finally, Gentille drew herself up and coughed out her remaining tears. "Sorry. I didn't mean to fall apart like that. I've wanted to tell you for a while now, and it just got all built up. And, no, Paul, you're not going to kill anyone. I hate my brother, but I can't have you committing murder on my account."

Gregorie touched her shoulder and said, "No matter what happens, you will not leave without your Mia."

Just like before, he experienced an internal connection to her, like they were two plants that shared the same pot, their roots intertwined. With this, his fangs settled back.

"Moving on," Paul said. "We're going to need a little insurance as we make our way back to the boat. And by insurance I mean wooden stakes. Two, maybe three, apiece. Or, as many as we can carry." He exhaled loudly through his nose. "It's likely we'll get jumped on the way, especially if this Reynaud character is serious about adding our French friend here to his nest."

Liam said, "I know where there's a stretch of old fence post we can break down."

"Perfect. Get that, and I'll make the necessary alterations. They have to be knife-sharp in order to penetrate the monster's heart." Smack-thump, he threw the orange ball against the bus wall. "In the meantime, Benicia, will you be able to retrieve the toddler?"

"Yes. She's in day care at this hour."

"And abducting her from day care will be no problem?"

"I won't have to abduct her. Don't worry, Paul, I know what I'm doing."

"Okay, great, just checking," he said. "I mean, if I took my kid to day care, I'd expect security to be a little tighter than any old person can walk in and—"

"Leave the day care to me," she said, "and I'll leave the vampires to you."

"How do you know so much about vampires?" Gregorie asked.

"Oh, you know, it's sort of a hobby of mine."

"He still reads comic books," Liam said, lifting one from the mess of stuff on the floor, the word *Morbius* on its blood-splattered cover.

"And you're sure we'll be able to get away?" Gregorie said.

"No, I'm *not* sure. I'm not sure at all," Paul said, serious as can be. "But I'd love to kick some vampire ass, so I guess I'm the best chance you've got."

Eighteen

Apparently the crime scene occurred just one block from the day care center.

Gentille decided she and Gregorie would pick up Mia alone so as not to draw the caregivers' undue suspicion. They would have to take a lender bicycle, as East Beach lay at the opposite end of the island. Gentille led the way to the racks that held the bikes and then, once again, pedaled Gregorie across town.

The nearer they came to the day care, the more people they encountered. They coasted alongside black-and-white cars (Gentille called them "police," those who uphold the law) and behind other people on bicycles, and those walking as well, all of them seemed in a hurry to get somewhere.

"I guess we don't have to worry about running into Reynaud over here," Gentille said. "There are so many police and other people nearby, surely he'll stay away."

Gregorie wasn't so sure that was true, even if Reynaud had killed those people.

They came to a complete stop in traffic. Several police in

black uniforms crowded into the area just beyond a large orange sign that read, "Detour."

"They've roped off the scene of the crime," Gentille said. "We'll have to go around the block."

She rode down the thoroughfare, came to the first left she could take, turned and then turned again. Soon they arrived at the lush, green front yard of a small white house decorated with red, yellow, and blue pictures of blocks with letters and numbers painted on them. A sign in the yard said, "Kiddie Academy."

Gentille held the bike while Gregorie dismounted. Now that they'd made it to the place where they'd pick up the child, he wrestled with a new level of concern. He wished they could hurry up and go to the boat. Time was passing like a stream, and he sensed that this was a bad thing. "Are you ready?" he asked.

Gentille pushed the front wheel of the bicycle into the rack, then stepped closer and faced him. "I'm really scared right now," she said.

"Me too," he told her.

"But I'd rather die than leave without her." Gentille shook her hands as if trying to shake the nervousness out of them. Then she bowed her head, perhaps to say a quick prayer.

"A child should be with her mother, and I know that you are a good mother, and that Mia should be with you."

She pursed her lips and touched his face. "You have such a kind soul."

He reveled in the compliment. "And I am sorry that I am a vampire."

"What? No, no, Gregorie, you're not. You're an angel of death, just like your mom always said."

He nodded, the warmth of satisfaction filling him. "I feel that I should kiss you now. For luck."

She laughed a little. "Okay."

He kissed her cheek.

She took his hand and squeezed it. "We are friends," she said.

"Yes," he agreed.

"You love Michaelangela."

He glanced up at the blue sky so crystalline after the prior day's storm. "My whole life I have loved Michaelangela."

"And now she has returned."

"She is not the girl I once knew. But I still love her, just as I love Maman and Guillaume and Saint-Suliac."

"And that is where we'll go, right? To France. Together?"

"Yes, we will go together," he said, though this was no longer his plan. Lying was the only way to get her to leave the island, he knew, and that was okay because he needed her and her child to get as far from him as possible.

There was relief in her smile. "I knew you'd come to your senses."

They continued down the path to the front door.

"I'll do the talking," she told him as he opened the door for her and entered what smelled mildly of both baby poo and flowers, as if the flowers were trying but failing to cover the unpleasant scent.

Beyond the entrance, a woman sat at a desk, her T-shirt and pants covered in part by a navy-blue apron with pictures of apples with worms coming out of them. She wore her gray hair short and curly, and peered through roundish glasses much smaller than Gentille's sunglasses. The sound of children singing came from the rooms beyond.

"I'd like to sign my child out for the rest of the day, please," Gentille said, lifting a pen from a cup and clicking the top a few times.

"You do, do ya?" The woman checked her wristwatch. "We just got everybody checked in. Is everything all right?"

"Yes," Gentille said with exaggerated pleasantness. "Everything is fine. I know it's early—"

"Only 7:30 a.m." The woman tapped her watch. "And what is your name?"

"Benicia Ayudante."

"So you are retrieving Mia Ayudante, I presume." The woman pressed her glasses up her nose before tapping her fingers over the board of little squares that sat on top of the desk. "Have you picked up before? I don't see your name on the family list."

"Yes, I have. Please call my parents."

Gregorie touched Gentille's hand and made a frown face.

Gentille said, "It's fine."

"I'll try the landline," the woman said.

Gentille said, "Perfect."

The beaded strings attached to the woman's glasses clicked against the U-shaped thing she brought to her ear.

Gentille took hold of Gregorie's hand as the woman dialed.

"This is a phone?" he couldn't help but ask.

She laughed, her face brightening. "You always know how to lighten the mood."

He supposed that was a good thing, and he supposed it was a phone too.

"Yes, hello, sir, we have a Benicia Ayudante here to pick up Mia. She's not on the list, so I'm calling to confirm." She adjusted her glasses and stared out the front window streaming with morning light. "Yes, she's here right now." She blinked. "Well, I don't know. Would you like to speak to her?"

She offered Gentille the phone. "Mr. Ayudante would like to speak to you."

Gentille's lips trembled, and she swallowed as if trying to prevent her fear from rising with her words. "Hi, Dad, I'm taking Mia for a few hours—" She paused. "Oh, it's you," her voice sunk into a less-friendly timbre. "I don't have to ask your permission." Gregorie heard the murmur of a voice coming through the phone. Then Gentille said, "Go right ahead. You know the agreement. I'm allowed seven days a year." She bit her bottom lip, and passed the woman, who was still sitting at the desk, a forced smile. Then she turned away from her and began to whisper fiercely: "You agreed to these terms, jackass. It doesn't matter that I didn't give you notice. If you don't do this for me, I'll go to the newspapers. As a matter of fact, we're not past the statute of limitations, and if I want to, I can do a lot more than alert the media." She stopped and listened. "Yes, I know about things like the statute of limitations, Eli, so I guess you better give your damn permission."

No sound came through the earpiece.

"Are you there?" Gentille said. "I don't have all effing day."

At this point, she had stretched the curls right out of the phone cord.

"You can agree to my having her this one day, or you can wait and see what kind of article comes out in the *Wodge Morning Times*. Do you think I care who knows at this point? I don't give a crap because *I* didn't do anything wrong. It's your decision, you pathetic little pervert. Are you going to give permission or not?"

A moment later she handed the phone back to the lady and said, "He would like to speak to you." Then she walked away and pulled at her top as if airing a blast of heat out of her shirt.

"Yes, sir," the woman said. "We'll get her all packed up and ready to go. Thank you, sir."

"She's going to get her," Gregorie whispered with glee before grabbing Gentille in a hug. They held each other, and Gregorie squeezed long and hard to brand the moment into his memory. Soon they would go their separate ways, and he wanted to make sure he remembered.

The woman returned holding the hand of a tiny child with coffee-and-cream skin, a brown pouf of hair with light streaks, and peachy cheeks. Gregorie had never seen anything so adorable. With tiny hands resembling soft-baked buns and miniature pink fingernails like the shells of the coquille, she put a spell on him at once.

Gentille plucked her from the ground and swung her in a circle. "I've miss you so much!" she said. The sound of giggles filled the room as Gentille covered the little girl with kisses.

When she put Mia back on the ground, Gregorie squatted to meet the child at her height. "Hello, little stinker," he said, and she reached out and planted her hand in his hair.

The woman in the apron took Gentille to get Mia's things from "the cubbies."

"She wants you to hold her," said Gentille over her shoulder as she followed the woman down the hall.

He lifted her, her little body and tender limbs light as a puppy in his arms. Then he bobbed her up and down, grinning at her button nose and buttery-soft complexion. Thoughts of Michaelangela leapt into his mind and took him off guard. They were the same thoughts he'd had when he once imagined marrying her and starting a family, having beautiful children who would look, he had assumed, a lot like Mia.

Still holding the child, he gazed out the wide front window that allowed a view of the road. To the right, a ways up, a yellow band marked an area that people were not allowed to go. A group of bystanders hovered but didn't pass through. Just beyond, some police moved about and others gathered. Gregorie wondered where Reynaud might be, and as he did, a young woman strode down the sidewalk in front of the day care, and a murky feeling of dread crossed like a shadow over his soul. He needn't see her face in order to know who she was. She wore a white dress down to her ankles, her wild brown hair trailing behind like wisps of wind. He continued to watch, holding his breath, as she crossed the thoroughfare to the other side. Unlike the girl he knew in France, she was otherworldly and gorgeous, graceful to a magical degree—and Gregorie's fascination with her could not be denied.

Oddly, the group of people she passed didn't seem to notice her at all. They moved out of her way without looking at her, as if she'd pushed them away with her mind. And then he remembered what she was, and a sudden paralysis came over him as he considered her power. She was like a celestial being making her way through the earthly world. The people standing there should have been in awe of her, perhaps they should have even run from her. But no one did.

She entered the area beyond the yellow band unhindered. The police, unbothered by her presence, stood mere steps from her, and not one of them tried to stop her.

Mia grabbed a handful of Gregorie's hair and pulled, ousting him from his transfixed state. Gentille was hurrying over while shoving a covered red cup into the bag at the same time. When she made eye contact with Gregorie's wonder-struck expression, she braced herself. "What's wrong?"

"Michaelangela," he whispered, relishing the sound of her name in his mouth. "She just passed by."

Gentille took in a sharp breath. She must have caught sight of Michaelangela's lithe figure just before she moved out of sight.

"Out," Mia demanded. "I want outside!"

Gentille extended her arms, and Gregorie passed her the impatient child. "Why would they be here?" she said. "There are police everywhere. Do you think she and Reynaud followed us?"

Gregorie continued to stare out the window, though

Michaelangela could no longer be seen. He wouldn't tell Gentille, but it took some effort not to run out the door after her. His mind knew what he wanted—to stay put—but his body wanted to join her, to hold her hand, to kiss her.

"Gregorie!" Gentille's voice hit him like a gong. "What's she doing here? Can you even hear me?"

He literally shook his head in order to clear it. "Reynaud must be nearby," he said. "I told you, he and I are connected. That's why I wanted you to leave without me." And now he was angry with himself for letting this happen. Gentille and Mia needed to go with Liam and Paul. He should have made them do it.

"We'll exit through the back," she said, grabbing his hand. "Come on."

She approached the lady with the gray hair and thick glasses. "Do you mind if we leave out the back door? We want to see the playground."

"Of course you can. We have the finest toddler apparatus on the island. All the children love it."

The woman led them down a hallway of doors and windows that opened to the many different classrooms in the building. At the end, a lit exit sign marked their destination. She opened the door for them. "Just be sure to close the gate when you're through. Can't have any of the little ones toddling out on their own."

"Yup, sure thing," Gentille said, finally letting go of Gregorie's hand.

They stepped down the short set of cement stairs and ran past a slide, a set of swings made for very small people, and several miniature vehicles on wheels. They opened the gate at the far side and continued into the woods beyond. Gentille spoke motherly assurance into Mia's ear: "We're just going to take a walk through the forest. We'll pretend we're wood elves! Won't that be fun?"

"Go straight to the boat," Gregorie said. "Do you have your phone? Press Paul's number and give it to me."

"I will go to the boat, but only if you promise to meet us there." She continued moving ahead as she passed the phone back without turning around.

"*Oui*, of course I will," Gregorie said.

A voice came through the phone. "Yo."

Gentille continued to move farther ahead.

"Paul?" Gregorie said. "Paul, can you hear me?"

"Loud and clear. Where you guys at? Did you get the kid?"

"We have her. But we think Reynaud is near. We saw Michaelangela, and we are going straight to the boat."

"Good plan. We'll meet you there."

"Okay, *bon*, *bon*. *Merci*."

"Yeah, man, let's stake those bitches," Paul shouted, adding a *whoop* at the end.

Gregorie stumbled in his mind. Did Paul want to stake Michaelangela as well? Why hadn't he realized this before? "*Reynaud*, you mean," Gregorie said. "We will kill Reynaud."

"Let's do it!"

Gregorie remembered Reynaud's monstrous strength and how he'd crossed the tall ship during the fierce storm and took Gregorie in his two enormous hands, exposing his neck before he'd so much as moved a muscle.

He would not be strong enough to stake Reynaud on his own, that much was obvious. He doubted any one of them—or even all four of them together—would be. But what could he do about that now? If they didn't make it to the boat before Reynaud found them, they would have to fight him. To avoid that, they'd simply have to make it back to the boat before Reynaud did. This was the plan. He prayed to Maman and Papi for luck and good timing.

"Paul, are you still there?"

"I'm here."

"If Gentille and Mia arrive at the boat before I do, take them across. Don't wait for me. Reynaud will not kill me. You must take Gentille and her baby to safety. Please promise."

"Yeah, I get what you're saying. Women and children first. But we can't leave you behind, man. We won't sacrifice you."

"But you don't understand," Gregorie insisted. "Reynaud will not kill me because I am an angel of death."

He may be small and weak, and still somewhat human, but he also had something Reynaud desperately wanted. He could save Reynaud's soul, and that gave him power. Some power. At least a little bit.

"An angel of death is just another name for vampire," Paul said.

Gregorie winced. How would he convince his friends to leave? How would he make them understand that there was no other option? None of them were safe. And Gregorie had lost so much already; he couldn't lose them as well. He stamped his foot. "You are wrong. All of you are wrong. Take Gentille and Mia across," he shouted. "Promise you will take them across!"

Nineteen

Cutting through the forest that paralleled the road, Gregorie jogged through the thin bodies of pines to catch up to Gentille and Mia. He gave her the phone, which she slipped into a pocket in her skirt. "We did it. We got away," she said, breathing with difficulty due to the extra weight of the child she carried. Sweat poured from her forehead and dampened her hair. "Do you remember how to get to the boat? In case we get split up? It's about a mile away."

"*Oui*. Past the restaurant. The Oyster Bar."

"That's right. We'll take the path that leads around back. Then down those steep sand dunes to the inlet. Do you remember?"

He did. "I hope the storm has not taken the boat out to sea."

"It will be there," she said, though a flutter of dismay crossed her face. "It better be there."

Mia began to fidget. "Down!" she said.

Gentille kissed her cheek and said, "Soon, baby. Soon."

Gregorie scanned the forest that surrounded them and sensed nothing, no one watching or following, so maybe she was right. Maybe they had gotten away. "If Reynaud shows up, keep going," he said. "Get to the boat. Paul and Liam will be there. I'll lead him away."

Her face had grown red with exertion, the bag with the baby supplies hung heavily from her shoulder and bounced into her backside as she broke into a jog. "Do you sense him? Is he following us?"

"*Non*, not now. But that doesn't mean—"

The footsteps arrived all at once as if Gregorie had been deaf for a time and suddenly regained his hearing. Someone walked on the path behind them. A glance over his shoulder confirmed it.

Reynaud trailed ten paces back.

"Go, Gentille! Go!" Gregorie cried.

Not knowing what else to do, he spun around and ran at Reynaud as fast as he could, hurling himself at the giant as if he were a mere mortal and not a vampire bulging with other-worldly muscle. They met in a full-body slam that rattled Gregorie's bones.

Reynaud remained motionless, unfazed by the impact and as unmoving as the foundation of a house. Gregorie suffered the same loss of control that occurs when one's stomach with-stands a bully's fist. He collapsed to the ground and, with great trepidation, gazed upward to meet Reynaud's unmerciful glare, the strong straight brows as treacherous as his canine teeth. Reynaud's grimace of disgust sent Gregorie's heart into a fit of palpitations.

"Take me," he said as soon as he could speak. "I am ready to leave with you. I'll stay with you forever. I was just . . . helping a friend get off the island."

"Helping a friend," Reynaud said, in a slow, threatening manner, "or endangering a life, maybe? I tried to tell you last night, *mon fils*, it doesn't matter what you do or where you go. I am not afraid of losing you. I am your maker. We are bound to one another now until the end of time. Fate will always bring you to my doorstep. I have never been more certain of that than I am now."

He bent over and placed his hands under Gregorie's arms, then whisked him off the ground and set him on his feet, pine needles falling from Gregorie's clothing. With a detestable scowl, Reynaud brushed the debris from the sweatpants Liam had given him. "What is this peasant attire that you wear?" he said. "We need to get you some real clothes."

"I wasn't leaving. I was sending her away. She's a mother."

"Mm." Like a jaguar on the prowl, Reynaud gaped fixedly into the distance, then eased back and sniffed the air. "She smells delicious. And she has the child with her now. That's tempting."

A swell of panic brought tears to Gregorie's eyes. His vision blurred as he scanned the forest for Gentille and Mia. Suddenly his canine teeth slid into their more-pronounced position. Was his body preparing for a fight?

Thankfully the girls remained out of sight—if Reynaud tried to take them, Gregorie didn't know what he would do. He would attack, of course, but what good would come of that? How could he possibly stop Reynaud? No, the answer was not to confront or fight. The longer he could distract Reynaud, the farther away Gentille would be, and the closer she would get to Paul and Liam.

"What have you done with Michaelangela?" he asked.

A subtle growl came from Reynaud, and he muttered, "You should be asking what she's done with *me*. It's been nothing but moodiness and agitation since she made your reacquaintance." He paused before adding, "I thought you said your friend was leaving the island. Can't say I blame her after what happened in town last night. It's a shame Wodge Island is proving to be such a dangerous place." He feigned disappointment. "But the ferry is that way."

Reynaud pointed in the opposite direction, his finger topped with a sharp, clay-colored nail. The finger and nail together looked like a bird's talon.

"She's not taking the ferry," Gregorie said. "Her family has a boat—the whole family will be there to see her off. Mother, father, aunts, uncles, brothers, cousins. Many people."

Gregorie hoped the thought of an entire family would be enough to dissuade Reynaud from pursuing a mother and child, but it only seemed to intrigue him. His brows lifted and pasty clay-like forehead creased. Funny how the sight of him changed from merely unattractive to downright horrible depending on the light and angle at which it struck him.

"Well, that's good news because I need a boat. You see, the police are searching for a large man dressed in black with a beautiful, goddess-like companion on his arm. And while Michaelangela has some mystical way of going unnoticed when she wants to, I cannot easily hide in plain sight." Reynaud stepped forward and gestured for Gregorie to proceed in the direction Gentille had gone.

Gregorie studied his maker's scaly complexion, his rheumy bloodshot demeanor, and jagged teeth. *Is this what I am to become?* A powerful man who uses his strength to do harm? The thought grated against his moral convictions.

"Lead the way, my scrawny mouse of a friend," Reynaud said.

They would *never* be friends. Reynaud didn't understand the concept, the meaning of the word *friend*.

"The forest comes to an end up ahead," Gregorie said. "Because they are seeking you, we'll have to turn. We cannot take the thoroughfare because, like you said, the police might see you and recognize you."

Reynaud nodded. "Sounds like a plan. Take me down whichever path you deem fit. But if it doesn't eventually lead to a boat, I promise you will be sorry."

"I will take you to the boat, and you can have it, but you have to make one more promise first."

Reynaud's eyes grew dead and bored. He blinked a couple of times before saying, "What is it I must vow to do, oh brave fledgling?"

"It's not what you must do, but what you must not do: promise you will not kill anyone else on this island."

He smiled as pleasantly as possible for a monster, then produced an equally agreeable laugh to go with it. "Is that all?"

Gregorie nodded solemnly.

"I'll make that promise, as long as you make one as well."

A cloud moved in front of the sun. The woods darkened and shadows lengthened. The leaves overhead rustled and chattered as if suddenly frightened. Gregorie's soul cowered within him.

"That you will stay with me. Travel with me. Be my family."

Gregorie didn't want any of that. But he would agree if it meant Gentille and the others' safety.

"Yes, okay," he said. "This way, please."

And on they went.

~

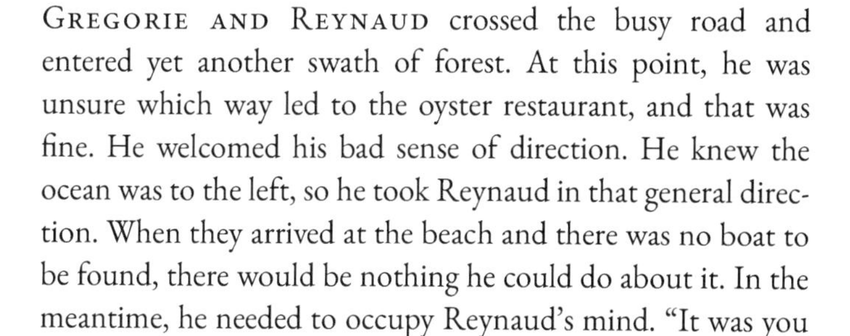

GREGORIE AND REYNAUD crossed the busy road and entered yet another swath of forest. At this point, he was unsure which way led to the oyster restaurant, and that was fine. He welcomed his bad sense of direction. He knew the ocean was to the left, so he took Reynaud in that general direction. When they arrived at the beach and there was no boat to be found, there would be nothing he could do about it. In the meantime, he needed to occupy Reynaud's mind. "It was you who killed the two people last night?" he asked.

"Two vampires arrive on an island," Reynaud said, "two

people end up dead. Surely you don't believe in coincidence." He sounded pleased with himself, as if he'd successfully told a joke.

"But why the police chief's wife and son? Everyone on the island knows them, and now all of the villagers want revenge. If you like spending time here, I think that was a mistake."

"Well, thank you so much for voicing your opinion." Reynaud flicked the back of Gregorie's head, sending a surprise stab of pain across his scalp.

"And I didn't kill both of them, for your information. I'm not a glutton."

Gregorie knew that he was, actually, a glutton, but he also knew what Reynaud was implying.

"Your precious Michaelangela has, shall we say, a certain type. Young, dark, and handsome," Reynaud said with a satisfied smirk. "She's far from innocent, and when she saw that young man, well, I was powerless to stop her. She simply had to have him. I don't know if you realize this about your former fiancée, but she possesses a strong will. She gets what she wants —even when I've advised against it. I suppose we all have our weaknesses." He paused there, making sure the implication took root.

Gregorie's vigilant heart once again shook itself awake. "Only because you made her into a monster," he said, surprised when the tips of his fangs bumped his bottom lip.

"Yes, well, three hundred years ago, she wanted to leave home, and I offered an opportunity. It's more than you did for her."

"She was just a girl. All teenage girls want to leave home. *You* took her from the people who loved her. I loved her. I wanted to spend my life with her."

"Love," Reynaud said with a scoff. "That's the thing humans don't get about vampires: we don't care about your petty, short-lived emotions. As for Michaelangela, I gave her the greatest gift this world has to offer. Thanks to me, she can live forever if she plays her cards right. You should be happy about that considering you have the same gift. Think of the possibilities, *mon fils*, all the lifetimes you can spend with her, thanks to me. Think of your special bond made even more special because you are my only children. You know that in time siblings make each other stronger, don't you?"

Reynaud may have considered infinite life a gift, but Gregorie never would. All this "gift" caused was heartache. Guillaume died believing his daughter longed to escape the home he and Beatrice had made for her. Because Gregorie had never returned from the West Indies, Guillaume would have lost all hope that Michaelangela would one day return. He would have died believing she'd been so miserable that she saw no other option than to leave.

Gregorie longed to go back in time, to visit Saint-Suliac, to explain to everyone that it had not been Michaelangela's intention to stay away.

The only good thing about forever was that it presented a possibility to one day get her away from Reynaud. "Our bond is strong because we loved each other," he said, "not because you gave us the same gift."

The vampire rolled his eyes. "That's not what I mean. I mean that you are vampire siblings. You make each other physically stronger. Not as strong as me, of course. But strong, or at least potentially so."

Gregorie didn't feel any stronger than he had before Reynaud and Michaelangela showed up at the cave—but maybe that had to do with the animal blood he drank. "Will I one day crave human blood?" he asked.

Reynaud scowled as if Gregorie's stupidity irked him. "You've survived for three hundred years in a box at the bottom of the sea. If you haven't craved human blood by now—"

"I haven't," Gregorie said, eagerly.

"But there have been animals . . ." Reynaud stared into the distance as if pondering this truth. "Can't say I haven't resorted to that every now and again. It comes with the territory, I'm afraid. And after the animals passed, I bet you sent their souls to the heavens, didn't you?"

Gregorie thought back to that first night when he came upon the lame deer so close to death. He'd gone peacefully without Gregorie's help. "No," he said. "The deer didn't need me. Some souls are born pure and die pure. His soared to the heavens upon angel wings."

Reynaud's face drooped with irritation. Jealousy, most likely. "I grow weary of our conversation," he said. "How much farther is this boat?"

Gregorie, leading Reynaud by just a few paces, pretended to study the area—as if he knew where they were. All of the trees looked the same. There were no landmarks, no buildings or signs to go by. "We're getting close," he said. For all he cared, they could have reached an entirely different island.

"You didn't know your father well, did you?" Reynaud said in an abrupt change of subject. "He and I were friends of a sort back when he lived in Mordes. Do you know Mordes? The underbelly of France itself. Sordid nightlife, drunks and their lost inhibitions everywhere. Back in the day, it was the perfect place for a vampire."

"I wouldn't know," Gregorie said.

Reynaud did not take offense. "You're a lot like your father in some ways."

Gregorie's insides curdled with the thought. Maman always said he was nothing like Marcel.

"Marcel Babin was a musician," Reynaud continued in a breezy, reminiscent tone, "and a gambler. Bit of a con man, like everyone else living in Mordes. In the end, he was more a gambler than a musician. Are you either of those things?"

"*Non*." Gregorie wished Reynaud would keep his information to himself.

"Oh, that's right. You were Maman's boy, through and through. There are much worse things you could have been, I suppose."

"Maman said Marcel and I shared only my brown eyes. And my hair."

"That is true. Marcel was a squirrely fellow who reeked of mischief. You are the spitting image minus that characteristic. He was about your size, with that thick tuft of hair falling into his shifty little eyes. Your father was not to be trusted, I'm afraid."

Gregorie hated his father for doing whatever bad things he'd done to make his mother feel he was not the type to light the moon. Why was Reynaud telling him all of this, anyway?

The vampire stepped ahead of him on the path and blocked the way so Gregorie stopped short. He kneeled down, put his hands upon Gregorie's shoulders and met his gaze the way adults do when telling children something important.

The sight of his face at such close proximity set Gregorie's nerves on fire. His heart stopped beating, as if knowing instinctively to hide itself. Web-like streaks of red marred the whites of Reynaud's round eyes, and his complexion, a morbid shade of beige, peeled in flecks around his ears and at the height of his forehead. "I just want you to know that Marcel, your father, was the one who told me where I could purchase quality handmade furnishings," he said. "Things like trunks made of exotic wood and fittings that would withstand the test of time and weather. . . . Perhaps even a dip in the ocean." He raised his brows, inviting Gregorie to put two and two together.

Gregorie's body grew stiff with rage. He wasn't sure he could move his lips in order to speak. "My father told you where you could get this?"

"That's correct. He led me to your small village. I'd never been to Saint-Suliac before, had never so much as heard of the place. He told me about Guillaume and his workshop. How he raved about his talent! After I heard all of that, of course I had to visit."

Marcel sent Reynaud to Saint-Suliac.

The thought stunned Gregorie to stillness.

"So, you see, Marcel is the one who brought me to your precious home." Reynaud seemed so pleased with himself. "He showed me the way to Michaelangela and eventually to *you*."

Gregorie's hatred for Marcel reared up like a startled horse, and once again his canines shifted into place.

"Of course Guillaume was more than happy to do business with me," Reynaud went on. "I offered him a fair price. Double what he was asking for, as a matter of fact. I've always been intent on sharing the wealth."

The urge to devour coursed through Gregorie's veins. "Did Marcel know what you were?"

"If you're asking whether he knew I was a vampire, the answer is as sure as the fangs peering through your pathetically thin lips right now. He most certainly did."

"*Non*. That cannot be true. He wouldn't—" Gregorie stopped. Could Marcel have done this? He didn't know what Marcel was capable of. Only that Maman disliked him immensely.

Reynaud patted Gregorie's head, then laughed so vigorously that his rancid breath spilled over Gregorie's cheeks. Gregorie feared the evilness in his breath might seep through his skin and poison his soul.

"Look into my eyes and tell me you don't believe it," Reynaud said. "What reason would I have to lie?"

The darkness Gregorie encountered in Reynaud's expression whisked him into a state of enchantment, his head spinning circles as his body filled with a cold, steady pulse. The blood in his veins spread a numb sensation through each limb and began to fill his chest. His fangs retracted, as if frightened back into hiding. He could not move, could not stop the vampire's ability to commandeer his body. Afraid for his life, Gregorie did the only thing he could do to break the connection: he closed his eyes.

Nothing changed at first. But as the seconds passed, he sensed a gradual withdrawal. A letting go. Soon, the sensation of numbness and cold gave way to his usual state: cool but not frozen.

When he opened his eyes again, Reynaud no longer knelt before him but had continued a short distance ahead.

"Hurry now," he told Gregorie. "Don't want to be late."

At the forest's end, the restaurant appeared. A sign with a picture of an oyster shell with a pearl in the middle stood amid the mottled shade of the trees out front. Hopefully Gentille and Mia had boarded the boat with Paul and Liam, and now steered toward the mainland. Gregorie had given them plenty of time to get ahead. Reynaud might kill him in a fit of rage when he found out there was no boat, but that would be better than living the rest of his life as a full-fledged vampire. No matter what, he'd find a way to die with a pure heart so that he could join Papi in lighting the moon.

All will be fine, he thought as a feeling of calm swept over him.

Proceeding through the oyster bar's parking lot, Reynaud remained behind him, rambling about things Gregorie would rather not hear. "I wish I could have been here when you finally broke free of the trunk. I suppose you dragged the bottom of the ocean inch by tiny inch, nudged along by the current, until finally you arrived close enough to the coast that the possibility of the chain becoming caught on something grew significantly—the anchor of a ship manned by a second-rate captain, perhaps. God knows there are plenty of those these days. The trunk must've dragged, maybe even pulled for miles, before it eventually dashed into some serendipitous rock and—"

Gregorie remembered the sudden thunderclap and tug of magnificent force. "It could have been!" he shouted. "I know my shell was dragged. I remember the sounds." The scratching and jostling and glugging. The trunk had crashed into something hard and unmoving, and broke apart just before he'd met with the water and experienced the long-lost freedom of movement. Where once he'd been the mollusk safe inside the shell, he became tossed into the wet world of the sea, reborn with arms and legs, his instinct telling him to swim up.

"When I reached the surface," Gregorie said, turning around so he could face Reynaud, "I saw a boat in the distance. I didn't know what it was at the time. It was white with colored flags and lights, very different from the ships I knew in Saint-Suliac."

"So you were caught by some drunken sailor's dragging anchor, then. And afterward you ended up wandering into my cave," Reynaud said. "I told you the fates brought you to Wodge Island so that we could meet once again."

Resisting that thought, Gregorie came up with a better one: perhaps the fates had brought him to the island so that he could meet with Michaelangela and help her regain her freedom.

The question was how?

"I am your maker," Reynaud said. "If you'd be so inclined, I could drain you again and properly fill you this time. My blood will nourish you, make you more like me. You'll no doubt bulk up, maybe even grow a few inches and—"

"And I will crave human blood and become a killer. *Non*, thank you," he said with disgust.

"You're a three hundred-year-old fledgling when you could possess the strength of four, five, six men. Don't you want to know what that feels like? When I was a younger man, still human, I was weak like you. I dreamed of becoming strong, of never needing to rely on anyone else, of never again being beaten or hurt. When given the opportunity to become something bold and fierce, I took it. Gratefully, I might add."

"And now you are worried for your soul," Gregorie reminded him.

Reynaud's upper lip curled into a snarl before flattening into a frown of obvious annoyance.

It had never occurred to Gregorie that long ago Reynaud had been an ordinary human. A *young* man. Apparently one that was not a giant, one that actually lacked strength. Was that why he looked forward to doing this for Gregorie? Because he knew what it was like to be physically small and afraid? Even if Reynaud's intentions were good, and not wholly selfish, Gregorie couldn't let it happen. As long as he had something Reynaud desperately wanted, he had power, and if Reynaud wanted to come out of this situation with his soul heading in the preferred direction, he'd have to honor Gregorie's wishes.

"If you ever drain me without my consent," Gregorie said, with a quiver in his voice, "I promise I will not save your decrepit soul. And worse, I will send it straight to hell."

Reynaud grumbled a bear-like growl that made Gregorie regret his bold words. He didn't know how to send a soul to hell, but then again, he had never tried.

"That's too bad," Reynaud said, sounding regretful. "For a second there, I thought we were becoming friends."

You thought wrong, Gregorie said to himself.

For now, being an angel of death ensured Gregorie's safety,

but he couldn't trust Reynaud not to lose control, not to accidentally drain him and make him drink his murderous blood in the midst of a fit of fury—even if it would cost him eternal damnation.

Gregorie knew what it was like to lose control. How desire could overpower logical thinking. And Reynaud flipped from kindly gentleman to furious monster at the drop of a hat. The best Gregorie could do as they approached the small cove was hope for the best and expect the worst. And he didn't like that one bit, because the worst involved harm coming to Gentille, Mia, Liam, and Paul, and he simply could not let that happen.

Twenty

The sound of distant waves arrived on salty breezes. Past the oyster bar, a moderate incline curved left and slid gently downward, allowing Gregorie to naturally gain speed and put a few more steps in between him and Reynaud. Soon enough those extra steps turned into several more, and Gregorie dug deep, shifting into a full-blown run. When he reached the top of the steep hill of dunes, maybe fifteen feet above the beach below, he leaped as vigorously as he could, getting air for a couple of seconds. His feet crashed into the warm, pliable sand, and he slid on his behind the last few yards to the flat expanse of the beach. As soon as his legs took their place underneath him, he ran.

In the distance to the left, waves rolled into the small inlet. High tide was upon them. The boat no longer bobbed where they had left it moored to the spindly sapling poking through the sand. He would have been so happy to find the boat gone, but it was there. On the far side of the cove, floating unmanned, it hovered dangerously close to some rocks, the rope dangling from its bow.

His friends had not left. Where were they? Why hadn't they gone?

And now Gregorie had accomplished exactly what he'd wanted to avoid. He'd led Reynaud to their meeting place.

The squeal of a young child held against her will rose up behind him. *Mia*. He spun around. A thick hedge of seagrass jutted from the foot of the dunes no more than twenty yards away. He ran to it. Where else could his friends possibly hide on this wide-open beach?

Meanwhile, Reynaud's deep, devious voice dropped down from the top of the dune: "You should not have run from me, Gregoire. I know you're here with that child and her mother, and . . . someone who smells as cowardly as you do. Do you think you can get away from me so easily?"

Gregorie rounded the row of seagrass, where he found Gentille, Mia, and Liam huddled together in a tight circle.

Gentille whispered, "Oh, thank goodness," as he joined them.

"You didn't leave," Gregorie said. "You were supposed to leave!"

A string of garlic hung from Gentille's neck, and the scent hit him like the queasiness that comes with the flu. He gagged but at the same time he was so relieved to see her that he couldn't help joining the three of them in their huddle.

After a moment, Gentille said, "The boat's too far out. We were afraid we didn't have time to get to it. We have Mia to worry about now." The child stretched and yawned, her head wobbling as she stuck her thumb in her mouth. "She's exhausted. It's probably her naptime."

"Where is Paul?" Gregorie said.

Liam shook his head. "He was right behind me on the way here, but when I slid down the dunes, I realized I was alone. Haven't seen him since."

"He'll be here," Gentille said. "Paul *would not* ditch us. He can be a real pain in the ass, but he'd never do that."

"Where are the stakes?" Gregorie said.

Liam pointed to a pile at the foot of the tall grasses. "Those are the ones he gave me," he said as he grabbed one and handed it to Gregorie. The tip had been whittled to an impressive point; the opposite end, sanded to a smooth hand hold. Maybe they would be able to stake Reynaud after all. Maybe, if they all ran at him at once, they could overwhelm him.

"We can't fight him without Paul," Gentille said.

"We might have to," Gregorie said.

"But what about Mia? I can't leave her alone." As she gazed lovingly at the toddler, her chin quivered. "Why did we think we could do this?"

"It's okay," Gregorie whispered. "I will take care of Reynaud. He wants me."

"Yes, you will take care of me, Monsieur Babin," Reynaud called from the top of the dune, his voice filling Gregorie with dread. "Get out here and fetch my boat. We had a deal. You give me the boat, and I won't kill your friends. Or have you forgotten?"

His demands shot painful venom into Gregorie's ears. "I really wish you had left," he told Gentille.

She inhaled deeply, then gazed at the toddler in her arms and trembled out an exhale. "She's so beautiful, isn't she?" She brought Mia's forehead to her lips and kissed her. The child continued to sleep.

Liam brushed Mia's cheek with his fingers. "I love you, Benicia," he said, in a sudden declaration that took Gregorie by surprise.

Gregorie turned away; it was the best he could do to give them some privacy.

"You know that, right?" Liam continued. "I've loved you for a long time now. I—I just wanted to make sure you knew."

Gentille swallowed and said, "Yes, I know. I'm sorry I couldn't tell you about Mia. I tried so many times but the words wouldn't come. I was afraid. I didn't know how you'd—"

"I wish you could have trusted me," he said, his voice soft with concern. "I would have helped you get her back."

"Well, I got her back myself, and I'm not going to lose her now. So we better grab those stakes and do whatever we have to do to get out of this together."

Gregorie turned back to Gentille. "You stay here with Mia, but take a stake. Take two." He reached over and grabbed another for himself as well.

Reynaud rounded the seagrass in a casual way, as if he were out for an afternoon stroll and not burning with the indignation of Gregorie's deceit. Dressed in his simple black pants and top, he may have passed for human had his upper body not vibrated with an aura of forbidding and his oversized hands not reeked of savagery. In all of his understated rage, Reynaud pointed his crusty finger, quivering with withheld fury, as he said, "Your plan is to stake me?"

Liam's complexion paled, and Gentille held back a scream as she placed her hands over Mia's precious ears. In the next second, Reynaud seized Gregorie by his neck and pulled him off the ground. Ruthlessly suspended, Gregorie withstood an almost unbearable pressure. The panic that would have done him in as an ordinary human didn't occur because he didn't need to breathe. *I am both dead and alive*, he told himself. *I can take it*.

"Do you actually think you can destroy me?" Reynaud's unmerciful voice threatened. "Well, what are you waiting for? Do it."

Gregorie had forgotten about the stakes in his hands. He

dropped them. Not because it was the smart thing to do but because Reynaud's grip on his neck had cut off control to the rest of his body. He strained to speak, his voice a whispery screech. "I was . . . saying goodbye . . . to my . . . friends. I . . . will . . . get . . . the . . . " He could say no more. A terrible compulsion to give up washed over him, and his eyelids drooped, the world darkened.

"Yes, you will get the boat, you pathetic piece of crap!" Reynaud said. "And then I will decide what to do with—"

"Release him!"

The words boomed from above as if God herself had spoken from a cloud-perch in the sky. The seagrass rattled in a chill wind, and suddenly Reynaud was gone.

Gregorie fell to the ground, his legs collapsing underneath him. He couldn't move. His bones and muscles failed to respond to his desire to rejoin his friends, all four of his limbs suffering painful pins and needles. With great effort, he scuttled back behind the seagrass, then sought a view of the top of the dune he'd leapt from only a few minutes before.

With the wind blowing her white cotton dress and alluring dark and light tendrils, Michaelangela stood atop the dune like a deity upon a pedestal.

Reynaud gazed up from below. "My darling, stop whatever foolish game you're playing, and get down here," he shouted to her. "Gregoire was about to fetch the boat for us, and we'll soon be on our way."

Michaelangela remained steadfast, a figurehead carved into the front of a ship, her white gown clutching her lithe body. "*You'll* be on your way," she said.

Reynaud would make her pay for that. He was not the type one told what to do, and Michaelangela had spoken to him as if he were a child.

A halo of violets fluttered around her head, and her complexion seemed to glitter as it caught the rays of the descending afternoon sun. She wasn't the girl Gregorie once knew, and he accepted that. He'd always love her, even if the girl he knew had long ago become something dark and forbidding. Underneath all of that, he believed, his best friend with the mischievous sense of humor remained.

"I don't play games," she said sadly, "and never foolish ones. I haven't played games since I was a girl in Saint-Suliac. You made sure of that, didn't you, Reynaud?"

"Can we discuss this matter at another time, sweetheart? We have a boat to catch." And then he called to Gregorie, "Get out here now, peon, and fetch the boat."

In the woods that backed up to the top of the dune, just yards from Michaelangela, a man with a black headband tied around his forehead skulked. Wearing an olive-green shirt and black pants, his beard secured in a braid that hung below his chin, he wielded a stake in each of his hands and set off in a run. At first Gregorie did not recognize this person as Paul, but of course that's who it was. He'd been waiting for the right moment to make his move. As Paul raised his weapons above his head and released a savage cry, Gregorie shouted, "*Non*, not her!"

As if she had eyes in the back of her head, she turned and snatched both stakes from his grip, then backhanded his six-foot frame in the same direction from which he'd come. Paul flew through the air, an echoing *ugh* dropping down from above when he landed out of view.

Gentille let out a gasp, and Liam put his hand on her shoulder. "He'll be okay," he whispered.

Gregorie hoped the forest's brush-covered ground took the sting out of Paul's fall, and he was glad the attempt to stake Michaelangela had failed.

Now she held one of Paul's stakes like a staff in her hand, radiating the confidence of royalty. "Leave them alone, Reynaud," she said.

"Or what? Am I to believe that you, too, will attempt to stake me?"

"I'm going to do worse than stake you."

Reynaud bowed his head and sighed, his upper body drooping with impatience. "My love, please, let's not argue. It's been a tedious day. Let's simply get on the boat and leave this place."

Over his shoulder, he shouted in a much gruffer tone: "Don't make me come over there, Gregoire, or I may just have to tear you limb from limb."

"If you tear me limb from limb, I won't be able to save your soul," Gregorie shouted back.

"I'm not going with you," Michaelangela said, regaining Reynaud's attention. "You will be the only one to get in the boat and leave."

The giant licked his lips in an impatient manner, his fangs gleaming in the late-afternoon light. "Are you giving me orders?" The cruel notes in his baritone chilled the air and inspired the hair upon Gregorie's arms to rise.

Gentille clutched Mia tighter, and Liam took them in a protective embrace.

"If you don't do as I say," Michaelangela's voice emerged cool and controlled, "I will destroy you."

"Okay, okay, stop this nonsense at once," Reynaud said. "You know that's impossible! Not only because I am two hundred years stronger than you but also because in your own way, you *love* me."

Gregorie smothered the sudden desire to defend her. She *did not* love him. She *could not* love him.

Michaelangela's fierce stare dared Reynaud to say more. "You don't really believe that."

"Either way," he said, "you can't kill me, but I suppose you are welcome to try."

"I don't need to kill you in order to destroy you. I don't need to touch you at all. . . . I can do it with my words."

"Your words?" Reynaud's brow drooped and the rest of his face fell. He rubbed his forehead, as if fatigued.

"Because I've never told you how I really feel about you."

"Can we *please* talk about this later, my dear?"

"I detest you, Reynaud." The sentiment hissed through the air like a winding snake sent to strangle what was left of his soul. "All of the lifetimes you've spent bringing me gifts and taking me around the world and pampering me with luxury—throughout them all I have detested you."

Reynaud appeared to have ingested something he wanted very badly to throw up. "Insults. That's all these are," he said, shaking a hand at her. "What has come over you? Are you showing off for your former boyfriend? Is that what this is about?"

"The day I met you, I loathed you," she continued. "When you were merely another customer of my father's. Poor, repulsive Reynaud with his club foot and sallow complexion. There is no finery that can improve your unattractiveness. No jewels that can buy your happiness. Over the years, I have watched your fear and desperation grow along with my own. Your soul, your poor, decrepit soul, what will become of it?" she teased in a singsong manner. "It's threadbare at this point, if it exists at all."

"Enough!" he shouted, and he dropped to his knees in the sand.

She shook her head in a piteous way. "You're going to hell, old man. Because there is only one place for beings like you *to* go. *No one* can save you from your hideous self. Not even an angel of death."

Reynaud drooped as if experiencing a sudden lack of strength. "Why, my love? Why are you saying these things? You can't mean what you say. You simply can't." He climbed the dune so fast it seemed as if he'd jumped to the top in one leap. Suddenly he stood before her.

Her eyes grew large, though she remained as sturdy as a wall and did not cringe or show fear in any way. "You can't hurt me," she said, her voice aquiver. "If you do, all of my power will transfer to Gregorie. You only have two children, remember?"

"That's a myth. Who told you that? Where did you hear such a thing?"

She smiled at him. "Rosaline told me."

"You're lying," he shouted, seeming to grow even larger as he stood over her. "You've never met my maker. And if you had, she would not speak with the likes of you."

"Except that she did," Michaelangela said before she shoved him. The strength of her action vibrated through the air, a blast of wind rustling the thick cluster of seagrass that hid Gregorie and his friends. Reynaud fell, as if he'd dove backward from the top of the dune. Gregorie thought he might break his neck on the landing, but like a cat, he managed to come down on his feet.

Michaelangela threw her halo of violets at him. They broke upon his chest, petals falling to the ground. As he observed the crushed blossoms, he said, "You're putting on a show for these children. That's all this is. This must have been Gregoire's idea. He asked you to say these things."

She threw back her head of wild hair and released a roar, part scream and part howl, an act of unbridled emotion. The sound shook the ground below their feet. When she was through, an eerie silence fell over the beach.

"I'll see you in hell," she said, the hatred in her eyes flickering like auburn flames.

Paul, who had risen from his sprawl a few yards away, charged once again, this time with the limb of a tree, some greenery still waving from its end. When he reached Michaelangela's position at the top of the dune, she had already taken off. Her body and its white gown rose like a dove in the air. For a moment it seemed she might continue to ascend, to fly into the sky and disappear in the waning light—but then she began to fall. The stake in her hands pointed at her chest so that when she connected with the ungiving earth below, it penetrated just the right place, piercing her heart.

Gregorie screamed, "*Non!*" and reached for her, as if he might catch her from where he crouched in hiding.

Next he was up and running. As he raced toward her, it became clear that the stake went straight through, protruding from the back of her body. The whole of her hung limp and skewered, and a flower of deep rose blossomed upon her white gown.

Gregorie carefully removed her body from the stake. With a gentleness reserved for loved ones, he turned her over as he dropped to his knees and laid her across his lap. The evil leaked out of her in the form of black-red blood seeping into the sand. Soon the sharp angles of her face softened; her cheeks plumped and eyes shed their otherworldly gleam, reverting to the earthly brown she'd been born with. Once again, she became the girl Gregorie had loved, the young woman pure of heart and intention, the one she was before Reynaud had turned her. His spirit rejoiced to see it, until her body relaxed into his embrace, and her eyes closed.

His heart sank at the thought of her end, but then her lids fell open again, her lips upturned the meagerest amount. She looked upon him with gentleness and admiration, and they shared the connection he remembered, the one that gave him warm tingles throughout his body. "I do love you," she said in breathy, weak words.

A surge of painful happiness filled him, and for one flashing moment he relived the plans they'd made, the excitement for their future, the love they had shared. All of it arrived within him like a great burst of thunder that lingered as it rumbled across the sky.

And then it was gone.

And so was she.

As Gregorie wept, he sensed her soul in turmoil, trapped inside of her body. He reached for her, praying for her to grab on. "*Mon coeur*, let me help you," he spoke to her internally.

Her soul circled her body with a gentleness so faint he wondered if what he sensed was indeed her or only his desire to find her, to help her. He waited and hoped and whispered encouragement until finally she grasped him with both hands. In his mind, they were back in Saint-Suliac, running barefoot through the courtyard, saving baby birds, learning English words, floating atop the gentle waves at the village beach, the blue sky stretching for miles above their heads. They played games together and splashed each other—her laughter was a song he knew by heart, and he basked in her presence, glowing with warmth and happiness. Together again at last.

Soon a rosy golden shimmer brightened the surface of her skin and warmed her complexion. Her inner beauty shined through, and Gregorie longed for her to stay, to live, to speak to him. But her soul ascended, a gentle cloud of light that hovered for a moment, then mingled with the air before the breeze from the sea blew in and took it away.

"*Je t'aimerai toujours*," he told her. I will always love you.

Gregorie fell back as a swell of euphoria overtook him. "Go with grace," he said. "Go with grace, *mon coeur*."

At that moment, a surge of power spilled into him as if upon the crests of ocean waves. His body became overwhelmed with a sensation of liquid energy as his limbs stretched and filled, and his chest expanded. He saw all the colors of the world as his heart rang out like a gong, each pulse a greater dose of strength. *Michaelangela's strength*, he realized.

His skin tingled under the last light of day, his ears rang with sounds near and far. He heard everything from the winds blowing in the heavens above to the baby breaths coming from Mia and the exasperated gasps of Gentille. Thinking of the mother and child caused his fangs to extend, for the power to gather in his arms, and for his hands to curl into protective fists. His body never felt so solid, so whole, so ready for a fight.

When Gregorie opened his eyes again, only one thought came to mind: *I will destroy Reynaud*.

Twenty-One

Reynaud's face was right there, hovering. His horrible breath and evil red-rimmed stare were a welcome presence, for Gregorie wanted nothing more than to end him. Still lying on the ground, still basking in the surge of potency that flowed through each of his limbs, he looked left and then right. A stake lay only an arm's length away. In the blink of an eye, he grabbed it, sat up, and pressed his fists into Reynaud's chest. He watched in awe as the giant launched up and back through the air.

Yards away, Reynaud landed on the ground with a bone-cracking bounce. The shock left him with a numb expression, slack with surprise. After a stunned moment, he laughed as if unfazed by this display of strength. "Lucky shot," he said with a spit.

I did that, Gregorie thought, and any fear that may have lingered in the dark recesses of his mind flared and turned to dust. This time he would do it: protect his friends and himself.

Gregorie sprang up and ran, the stake's edges cutting into the palm of his grasping hand. He gained speed with each stride as he dug deeply into the newfound strength in his thighs and calves. The thrum of power drumming through his limbs resembled the sensation he'd felt when he drank blood. With Michaelangela's power coursing through his veins, he could do anything. He leaped through the air and raised the stake overhead, then brought his arms down with finality as his body descended. *Ka-thunk!*

He'd aimed at the vampire's heart and thought he'd struck the target.

At the last fraction of a second, however, Reynaud had rolled to one side and eluded the blow. The stake entered his chest and exited his shoulder at an angle. Like a skewered fish, the monster flopped as if boneless. He settled into a fetal position in the sand and released a deep-throated moan.

Gregorie backed away and eyed him with caution. Very little blood had spilled, and the lack of movement could have been a trick. He doubted this would be Reynaud's end.

A moment later, he sensed Gentille and Liam standing beside him, their fragrant garlic necklaces causing a wave of nausea. Gentille must have left Mia sleeping behind the seagrass. Paul came up from behind and said, "He ain't dead."

"He's hurt, at least," Liam said. "Wait . . . Is he shrinking?"

"Let's hit him again!" Gentille's enthusiasm oozed like a sore through Gregorie's mind. Wickedness wasn't her style, and he didn't like the way Reynaud seemed to bring it out of her. The fight needed to end, and he needed to be the one to end it.

"I'll do it," he said. That's when he noticed that his new protruding fangs changed the way he spoke. Both Gentille and Liam fixed their attention on him at the same time because surely they had noticed too, though neither commented.

"Dude, it's just your canine teeth," Paul said. "No worries."

But Gregorie *was* worried. Not only because his fangs were out but also because he was hearing the four of their human heartbeats in his ears. *Ba-boom, ba-boom, ba-boom*, and suddenly it became a lot harder to focus on killing Reynaud. He thought of the blood coursing through his friends' bodies —and little Mia's—and a tingle rose up from his belly. A tingle not unlike hunger. Desire . . .

Arrêtes! he scolded himself. Stop!

Gregorie grabbed a stake from Liam and ran at the unmoving mound that was Reynaud. For a flicker of a moment, he considered biting the vampire, the thirst for blood still very much present—and this inclination broke his concentration. Just as he leapt, Reynaud's arm rose, and his still-sizable hand opened and closed around Gregorie's slender neck. Before Gregorie knew what had happened, Reynaud had flipped him onto his back and hovered over him like a jaguar entranced by its prey.

"You may be stronger now, and I may be weaker," he said with understated rage that vibrated in Gregorie's ears, "but you're not ready for the likes of me, fledgling."

It was like staring into an animal's mouth. Reynaud's horrible fangs came at him, and Gregorie cowered in response to the stab wounds that penetrated his neck. He remembered the feeling well. Gentille's scream sliced through his mind and just as quickly faded as Gregorie once again met with a silence that drowned out the wind and ocean waves and . . . everything he knew.

A white light entered his mind, slowly growing brilliant as it washed out the gray of the ordinary evening sky. He relaxed, and as he drew back, he sensed death nearby. A gull cried out, and a moment after that he heard the sound of footsteps in the sand. Maman walked up the beach toward him. She wore one of her blue dresses and the highlights in her brown-gray hair sparkled like silver. The sun shone brightly here as it always had in Saint-Suliac. "What are you doing, *mon fils*?" she said as if surprised to see him. "Oh my goodness, Gregorie, close your mouth right now. You know that you cannot drink the blood."

Gregorie did as he was told.

"*Bon*. You were always such a good boy." She smiled as she continued on her walk, moving away much faster than he would have liked. "You shouldn't be here," she said, her voice becoming watery and distant, "but I will see you in the afterlife."

Ka-thunk.

Reynaud let out a horrible scream, and Gregorie lay back in the sand. As Maman's presence faded, he reached out in an attempt to grab it by its shirt tails. The wind caressed his face, and ocean waves kept time in the distance.

"Got him!" Gentille shouted. "Now you, Liam. Go, go!"

Ka-thunk.

Gregorie blinked and his vision returned. Reynaud lay under the evening sky, just a few feet away. Three stakes impaled his chest. The vampire turned his head and met his gaze. His expression imparted sadness, or so it seemed until his voice slipped into Gregorie's ear in the form of a hiss: "You can't kill me," he said.

Gregorie flinched and, just at that moment, realized someone applied pressure to the wound on his neck. "Hey, hey, calm down, I gotcha, buddy." It was Paul. "No way were we gonna let that bastard give you another dose of his evil swill. Smart move to close your mouth, though."

Reynaud turned away once again, and Gregorie watched Paul stand and then grab a stake from the ground. Next he ran at the unmoving mound and let loose a wild man cry. *Ka-thunk!* The fourth stake had found its final resting place.

"One from each of us," Gentille said. "You think it will do?"

The monster lay still at this point, wafts of smoke rising from his body. The three friends inched closer so they could better observe, but Gregorie stayed back. Reynaud was like a log from a fire that had heated up and glowed but had not burned all the way through. Too big for his dwindled body, his clothing hung from his limbs like a blanket. The skin upon his hands appeared parched and scaly.

Above them, the moon took its place as the retreating sun unfurled a soft sky blanket of light and dark gray.

Gregorie sat up, the life returning to him, his power reawakening. The wound upon his neck had already closed up and smoothed over. He no longer heard the beating of his friends' hearts, and for this he was grateful. He stood and joined them.

"Did you feel his soul leaving?" Liam asked.

He hadn't sensed Reynaud's soul at all. Perhaps it was true that Reynaud couldn't die. He was so old and well fed, so strong. "I don't think he's dead," Gregorie said.

Mia cried out from behind the seagrass, and Gentille ran to her, the sand kicking up behind her feet.

"You and Gentille must get in the boat with Mia and get out of here," Gregorie told Liam. Before his friend could ask any questions, Gregorie ran into the water, dove in, and swam as fast as he could to the place where the boat bobbed. He reached the rope that once tied it to the sapling, and tugged the vessel back to the shore, pleased by how easy it was to do.

Liam and Paul waited for him in the surf, small cresting waves breaking upon their knees. When he reached them, he handed the rope to Paul, the boat itself at least fifteen yards away, in deeper water. Gentille held Mia high upon her chest as she approached them. "Come on, I'll help you," Liam told her, and the two of them waded in together. He swam to the stern and pulled down the small ladder on the port side, then climbed into the boat first so he could assist.

In the meantime, Gregorie ran back to the foot of the dunes where Michaelangela's body remained. Like Reynaud, she had shrunken in size, becoming more like a body that has decomposed than a young girl who has passed before her time. As he lifted her, something like a stone dropped upon his foot. He bent over to find her obsidian ring, black as midnight. The ring he and Maman had given her for her seventeenth birthday. It warmed the palm of his hand, and as he slid it onto his finger, the metal seemed to clutch him.

He carried Michaelangela's fragile body, wrapped in its white cotton gown like a shroud, to the boat.

By this time Gentille had found a life jacket to put on Mia, and she was rummaging in the compartment where they'd left the key the prior day.

"What are you going to do with Michaelangela?" Paul said, and Liam observed Gregorie from the boat in wait of his answer.

"We often swam together at the beaches in Saint-Suliac," Gregorie told them. "She would appreciate a burial at sea."

Liam opened his mouth to speak, probably to explain why that was a bad idea, but Gentille came up behind him and said, "Of course we will."

Gregorie held the body overhead as he swam to them. Gentille and Liam reached over the side, easily pulling Michaelangela into the boat and laying her on the floor.

"Say a prayer for her when you're halfway to the mainland," Gregorie told them, "and tell her goodbye for me."

Gentille whipped around. "You're not coming with us?"

He couldn't go with them. Not until he knew it would be safe for them to be near him. He hated that it had to be this way, that he didn't trust himself, didn't trust his vampire body or his protracting canine teeth, or his ability to hear human heartbeats. He hated that he lusted after the blood of animals, and he couldn't bear the thought of one day losing control in the company of his human friends. *Non*, he couldn't go with them. It was out of the question.

"France isn't for me," he said. "Not now. Not yet."

"You promised," Gentille said, panic welling in her voice. "We were going together."

"I think you know why I can't." He paused to glance at Mia, belted to her seat.

Reluctant, Gentille followed his line of sight.

"You will love Saint-Suliac," he said, the sadness deepening his voice. "And you should be with Liam. He will be a good father."

She nodded, blinking away her tears.

He reached out his hand, and she took it, her warmth familiar and comforting. "One day, I will visit," he said. "We'll have a picnic at the cemetery, with Maman."

"Yes, but don't take too long. I'm going to miss you." She put a kiss on the top of his hand and then let go.

"Take care, buddy." Liam waved. "I know you're doing the right thing."

"Uh, while we're saying our goodbyes," Paul broke in from where he stood like a moor for the boat. "I have to say mine as well."

"What? Don't be ridiculous, Paul. Get in here," Gentille said.

"Are you serious? You seriously think I could survive in France? Look at me! I barely belong in the woods. I'm a frig-gin' cave man. You've told me a million times!"

"Okay, okay," Gentille said with a laugh. "No, I can't see you in France."

Liam cracked a smile.

"Besides," Paul said, "I don't want to barge in on the family thing you've got going."

"Goodbye, Paul. I'm hugging you goodbye right now," Gentille said. "You're not half as bad as you think you are."

"Are you kiddin' me? I'm the baddest of the bad. I'm a vampire slayer. I slayed today!"

"Bye, man," Liam said. "Take care of the bus."

"Yeah, yeah. See ya, wouldn't want to be ya," Paul said with a sad droop in his eye.

He threw the rope at the boat, and he and Gregorie watched Liam reel it in. Then the two of them stepped backward through the surf as the family began its journey, their vessel etching a trail across the water, the light of the moon bouncing off the crests in the sea. While Liam steered, Gentille held Mia on her lap and stared back at them, waving one last time before the sight of them faded into darkness.

In silence, Gregorie and Paul walked up the beach.

When they reached Reynaud, Paul put his hands on his hips and said, "So, what should we do with this beast?"

"I have an idea," Gregorie told him.

"Cool," Paul said, using his foot to give Reynaud a small kick. "Can't wait to hear it."

"Grab his feet," Gregorie said. "We must take him back to the cave."

As Gregorie and Paul maneuvered Reynaud's shrunken body through the narrow entrance of the cave, Gregorie thought of Gentille and Liam, and filled with the satisfaction of knowing that they and the baby were safe. Once inside, he and Paul placed the body on the ground. While Paul used his phone's flashlight to find the torch and light it, Gregorie went through Reynaud's pockets and came up with the key to the trunk's heavy metal lock.

Working in silence, they folded the once-giant vampire at the waist and fit him into the box that Guillaume built. With a bit of persuasion, the top closed and Gregorie wrapped the chain around it. He then secured the lock and handed Paul the key.

"I still can't believe he fit in there," Paul said as he put the key in his pocket.

"*Oui.*" Gregorie noted Paul's necklace of garlic, which still nauseated him. He gagged, and Paul said, "Oh, sorry, man, I guess I can take this off now." He was about to pull the necklace over his head, but Gregorie said, "*Non*, don't."

Paul stopped, then eyed him with understanding and let the necklace remain.

"You are sure that it will take him a long time to heal?" Gregorie asked.

"We're talking years, dude, many, many years," Paul said. "I've done extensive research—and not just comic books. I never told Liam and Benicia because they would have thought I was a grade-A nutjob, but the truth is I've spent a good many hours at the library reading about this stuff. You'd be amazed how many books there are on vampire folklore. I mean, if they awarded PhDs for this kind of thing, I'd definitely get one." He stroked his beard.

"Good, that's good," Gregorie said. "I believe you."

"Trust me when I say it will be decades before Reynaud is back on his feet. Probably longer. We staked him *four* times. I can't believe he survived. And he's locked in a trunk. Unless a rat scratches its way through its wall—an unlikely event considering how dense mahogany is—he has no means of obtaining blood. Without blood, it will take him forever to so much as stand. And that's a far cry from breaking a metal lock and chain. My guess is it will be a century before he even wiggles a finger."

"Good. That's good," Gregorie said. "You also said you wanted to move into this cave, but you won't, will you?"

Paul crossed his arms over his chest and observed the space around them. "This really is the best spot on the whole damn island, but I think I'll stay in the bus. It's cool knowing

Reynaud is safely stowed, but I don't need to be his roommate."

Gregorie was glad to hear it. He didn't like the thought of Paul living so close to Reynaud, even if he would require centuries to heal. Because . . . what if he didn't?

"Besides, it would be a royal pain in the ass to move stuff in here," Paul said. "I still can't figure out how that trunk made it through in one piece."

"There must be another way," Gregorie said.

Paul tipped his head back. "Maybe through the top?"

Gregorie looked up and a ray of moonlight caught his eye. "It is possible," he said.

"So, what about you," Paul asked. "Where will you go?"

While Michaelangela had been the one who wanted to see the world, Gregorie had only wanted to make a home near his mother. But maybe it would be nice to see other places. Wodge Island was too small to settle down in, even for a reluctant vampire. While he wouldn't draw attention—he wasn't beautiful like Michaelangela or hulking like Reynaud—he couldn't risk someone seeing him drink from a dying deer or a tub of fish. He imagined going someplace with trees. Miles and miles of them. And wildlife. Flowers and moss, mushrooms like he used to gather in Saint-Suliac. He'd always loved the woods back home, and the excursions he and Maman took in search of ingredients for her healing incantations.

"Do you know a place that has forests as far as the eyes can see?" he asked.

"That would be Canada," Paul said without pause. "Some people even speak French there. It's not too far either. Once you make it to the mainland, you can probably hitchhike. But you'll have to cross the border."

"Will this be difficult?"

"I don't suppose you have a passport?" Paul waved his hand, pushing the question away. "Don't worry. I'll talk you through it. Small guy like you shouldn't have a problem finding a fence to crawl under."

So that was it. Gregorie would go to Canada. He'd live among the trees and the animals until he understood himself inside and out. Until he was sure that he could control himself and trust his body not to override his mind. He would dwell in the fresh air and sunlight, and never drink the blood of a human being.

Gregorie was not a monster.

And one day his soul would light the moon.

Thank You

What would authors do without readers and reviewers? Thank you so much for picking up *Staked: A Vampire's Tale,* Book 1 in the Angel of Death series. I hope you enjoyed reading it as much as I enjoyed writing it. If you did, please leave a rating or review on your favorite book-centric website or platform. Leaving a review is like recommending a good book to a friend.

Subscribe to www.AuthorKimCatanzarite.com for news, giveaways, and updates on what's coming up next, including Book 2 in the Angel of Death series.

If you are a blogger and/or reviewer, please feel free to contact me at www.AuthorKimCatanzarite.com with questions, photo requests, or interview and guest blogging opportunities. I will be more than happy to help any way I can.

Acknowledgments

I thank my family first and foremost because they are the ones who make all of this possible. Joe and Jupe, you mean the world to me. Thank you for reminding me to eat dinner—and to occasionally step away from my desk.

For my mother, who taught me to remain flexible and never stop learning; for my father, who told me that if I wanted a piece of the world, I'd have to go out there and grab it; for my sister, who always makes me laugh, gets me to the beach, finds cool stuff for me to buy, and enjoys breakfasting as much as I do. *Three Birds, forever!*

To my group of die-hard supporters: Ron Skelton, Annette Masters, Debra Dynes, Lisa Hopwood, Patricia Olson, Laura Mahal, and John Remington. I'm looking at all of you and feeling grateful.

To my many betas and proofreaders over the years, thank you for being part of my process. Thank you in particular to Jenn Chastka.

To Tricia T. LaRochelle, I appreciate all you have done for me and my books. From the bottom of my heart, thank you.

Finally, to my readers, I love hearing from you! Enormous gratitude for picking up my book and reading it. Thank you for your kind words and your reviews, and for joining Gregorie on this adventure.

Last, to my furry friends, Lainey and George, I have failed to thank you in the past, but you, too, play an important role in my writing life. Please stop reminding me that in an hour it will be time for you to eat. I promise that I am well aware.

About the Author

Kim Catanzarite grew up in northern New Jersey reading Anne Rice novels and watching *The Lost Boys*. She tapped into her creative writing obsession while attending Skidmore College and has never looked back. She lives in New Jersey with her husband and daughter.

Made in the USA
Middletown, DE
07 October 2023